HERGÉ
★
THE ADVENTURES OF
TINTIN
★
RED RACKHAM'S
TREASURE

LITTLE, BROWN AND COMPANY
New York   Boston

This edition first published in the UK in 2007

by Egmont UK Limited

Translated by Leslie Lonsdale-Cooper and Michael Turner

Red Rackham's Treasure

Renewed Art copyright © 1945, 1973 by Casterman, Belgium

Text copyright © 1959 by Egmont UK Limited

The Seven Crystal Balls

Renewed Art copyright © 1948, 1975 by Casterman, Belgium

Text copyright © 1962 by Egmont UK Limited

Prisoners of the Sun

Renewed Art copyright © 1949, 1977 by Casterman, Belgium

Text copyright © 1962 by Egmont UK Limited

www.casterman.com

www.tintin.com

TRANSLATED BY LESLIE LONSDALE-COOPER AND MICHAEL TURNER

Little, Brown Books for Young Readers is a division of Hachette Book Group, Inc.

The Little, Brown name and logo are trademarks of Hachette Book Group, Inc.

First US Edition © 2009 by Little, Brown Books for Young Readers, a division of Hachette Book Group, Inc.

Published pursuant to agreement with Editions Casterman.

Not for sale in the British Commonwealth.

Little, Brown Books for Young Readers

Hachette Book Group

237 Park Avenue, New York, NY 10017

Visit our Web site at www.lb-kids.com

ISBN 978-0-316-35814-9

18

SC

Printed in China

RED RACKHAM'S
TREASURE

THE ANCHOR

BAR

'Morning.

BAR

Ahoy there! ...
Bill! ...

WHITE

Hello, George! How's
yourself? ...

Not so bad. And you?
Still a ship's
cook?

Still the same. I'm sailing aboard
the SIRIUS in a few days, with
Captain Haddock and Tintin.
Know them?

Tintin? ... Captain Haddock? ...
I certainly do. There's been plenty
of talk about them - over that
business of the Bird brothers.* But
the SIRIUS - she's a trawler, isn't
she? Are you going fishing? ...

Yes, but it's not ordinary fish
we're after, it's treasure!

What's that you say?

Well, it's like this ... There's a treasure
that belonged to a pirate, Red Rackham,
who was killed long ago by Sir Francis
Haddock aboard a ship called the UNICORN.
Tintin and Captain Haddock found some old
parchments ...

... written by Sir Francis ... who escaped
from the ship ... They know just where
the UNICORN sank and ... I'll tell you the
rest later. These walls have ears.

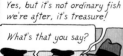

* See The Secret of the Unicorn

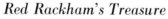

Red Rackham's Treasure

THE forthcoming departure of the trawler *Sirius* is arousing speculation in sea-faring circles. Despite the close secrecy which is being maintained, our correspondent understands that the object of the voyage is nothing less than a search for treasure.

This treasure, once the hoard of the pirate Red Rackham, lies in the ship *Unicorn*, sunk at the end of the seventeenth century. Tintin, the famous reporter—whose sensational intervention in the Bird case made headline news—and his friend Captain Haddock, have discovered the exact resting-place of the *Unicorn*,

Mr Tintin? . . .

Yes.

Mr Tintin. I see from this morning's paper that you are going to try and find Red Rackham's treasure. Is that so?

Yes, it is. But . . .

Good. In that case I shall accompany you! . . . As for the treasure, I shall be satisfied with a half share . . . Here is my card . . .

Is . . . is that really your name? . . .

So it seems, young man.

Look, Captain . . .

Blistering barnacles!

RED RACKHAM

But, if I'm not mistaken, sir, your name is simply Rackham. 'Red' is just a nickname. In which case I see no connection between you and Red Rackham the pirate . . .

RRRING

Mr Tintin? . . . I demand my share of the treasure! . . . I am Red Rackham's sole descendant! . . .

He's not. I am!

He's not. I am!

It's me!

Don't listen! I'm the one!

I am! And here's my family tree!

5

Leave this to me! We'll soon see if there's a real Rackham among that crew!

You're all descendants of Red Rackham are you?

Good! Well, I'm descended from Sir Francis Haddock, who killed Red Rackham in single combat . . . and blew up his ship . . . And there are times . . .

. . . when my ancestor's fighting blood begins to boil!

Avast, freshwater pirates!

What's going on up there?

What a stampede!

Like a lot of wild elephants!

A real herd of elephants!

To be precise: a real herd of elephants!

And there are your records, fancy-dress freebooters!

There you are. That's got rid of that gang of thieves!

RRRRING

Another?

Wait, I'll go . . .

Is that you Tintin? . . . It's us, Thomson and Thompson. Could you give us a hand? . . . A wild elephant dropped something on our heads.

!

Come in; we'll see to that . . .

RRRING

?

I'd like to speak to Mr Tintin.

Why? . . . No doubt your name happens to be Red Rackham?

Yes?

No, I'm asking you if you're called Red Rackham . . .

Oh?

WHAT'S YOUR NAME?

Please speak a bit louder. I'm a little hard of hearing.

YOUR NAME!

Gone away? . . . What a pity! Never mind. I'll come again. I particularly wanted to speak to Mr Tintin himself . . .

I'm Tintin. What do you want?

Ah, Mr Tintin! . . . They told me that you were away.

I'm delighted to meet you. My name is Calculus; Cuthbert Calculus.

Oh?

No, Calculus, Cuthbert Calculus. Mr Tintin, I understand you are setting off on a search for treasure. That's nice. But have you considered the sharks?

The sharks?

No, young man, I'm talking about the sharks. I expect you intend to do some diving. In which case, beware of sharks!

But . . .

Don't you agree? . . . But I've invented a machine for underwater exploration, and it's shark-proof. If you'll come to my house with me, I'll show it to you.

I'm very sorry but . . .

No, it's not far. Less than ten minutes . . .

I'm afraid I'm very busy and I . . .

Why of course. Certainly these gentlemen may come too.

It's no good. There's no time! NO TIME!

Good, that's settled. We'll go at once.

I'm so glad you agreed to come!

Please don't mention it.

No, Calculus, Cuthbert Calculus.

You see, here we are. One more floor . . .

It's in here . . .

Yes, that's a new device for putting bubbles in soda-water . . .

And that's a clothes-brushing machine.

Not a bad gadget, eh?

8

No, a clothes-brushing machine. It's one of my latest inventions.

RRRR ☆ OUCH

OW

OOH

The clothes are sucked into the middle of the machine, where they have a stiff brushing for half a minute. Then they come out, as good as new . . .

Billions of bilious blue blistering barnacles!!

Let me go! I'll tell him what I think of his practical joke!

You're going to buy me a new outfit, do you hear?

That? . . . Yes, it's for brushing clothes.

But this is even more ingenious. Because I have so little room and my bed gets in the way . . .

. . . I designed the wall-bed.

You Bashi-bazouk! Look what you've done now!

You bragging nitwit, you! Look!

How do I close it up again? There . . .

Between ourselves, I wouldn't have expected such childish pranks from them. They looked quite sensible . . .

And here's my apparatus for exploring the sea-bed.

As you can see for yourselves, it's a kind of small submarine. It is powered by an electric motor, and has oxygen supplies for two hours' diving . . .

Now I'll show you how the apparatus works . . .

? CRACK

I can't understand it! . . . It's sabotage! No sir, I said it's sabotage! . . . Someone has sabotaged my machine!

We are extremely sorry, Professor Calculus, extremely sorry, but your machine will not do.

For two? You'd like a two-seater?

No, Professor Calculus, I said your machine won't do for us!

Oh, good!

Well, gentlemen, that's agreed. I'll make another smaller one. It will be ready in eight days' time . . .

Some days later . . .

Well, we're all ready to start - at least, if we can find a diving-suit. I've spent three days hunting through marine stores, and I still haven't unearthed one.

I say, look there! Great snakes! Let's go and see . . .

FOR SALE
Complete Diving Equipment, as new

We'd like to see the diving equipment, please.

The diving-suit? Please follow me.

There . . .

Beware, young fellow, beware! Money is the root of all evil!

?

Why . . . why do you say that?

Why? . . . Because I see that you intend to go treasure-hunting . . .

You see that? Where can you see it?

I read it I your face.

In my face? . . . But . . . but . . . what's unusual about my face? Tintin, can you see anything?

Well, I . . .

Blistering barnacles!

It's horrible! . . . What's happened to me? . . .

Nothing, Captain! It's just that you were looking in a concave mirror! And here's a convex one!

Thank goodness!

But here's another mirror . . . I'll just reassure myself!

Oh!

Seven years of bad luck!

And two pounds for the mirror!

You can take it from me: I'm telling you the truth: there's no such thing as buried treasure nowadays . . .

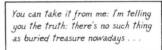

Never mind that. How much is the diving-suit?

Ten pounds.

All right. We'll have it collected this afternoon. Shall we go, Captain?

Remember what I said, my lad. You won't find any treasure!

Next day . . .

SIRIUS

Good morning, Captain. All well?

No, bad!

Yes, bad. Very bad . . . I'm ill . . . 'Flu, I expect . . . And I've been thinking . . . I . . . well . . . briefly, to put it in a nut-shell, I'm not going!

!

You can't be serious!

Perfectly serious. I'm not superstitious, but to break a mirror on the eve of a voyage . . . No, definitely, I'm not going!

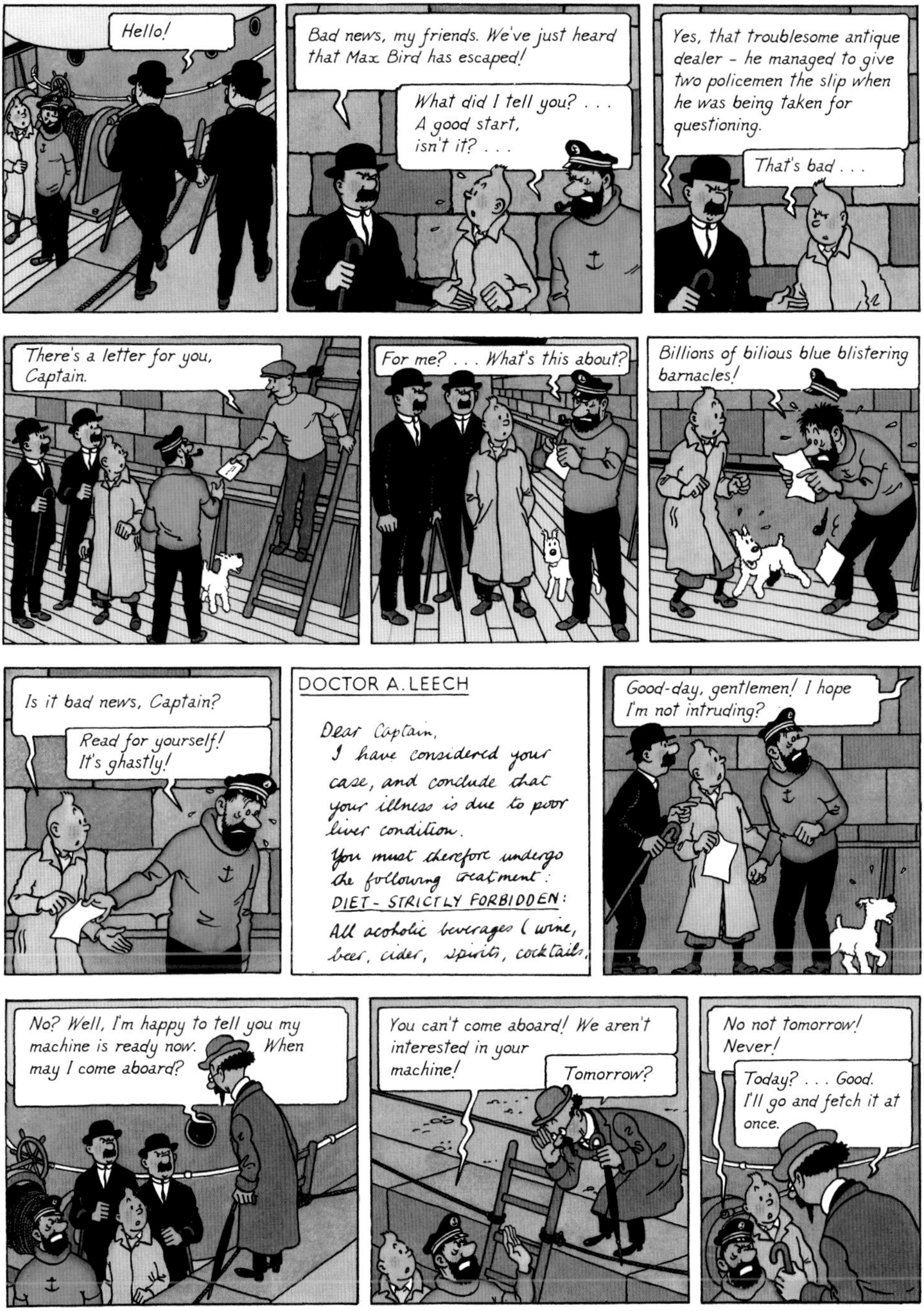

Hello!
Bad news, my friends. We've just heard that Max Bird has escaped!
What did I tell you? . . . A good start, isn't it? . . .
Yes, that troublesome antique dealer – he managed to give two policemen the slip when he was being taken for questioning.
That's bad . . .
There's a letter for you, Captain.
For me? . . . What's this about?
Billions of bilious blue blistering barnacles!
Is it bad news, Captain?
Read for yourself! It's ghastly!
DOCTOR A. LEECH
Dear Captain,
I have considered your case, and conclude that your illness is due to poor liver condition.
You must therefore undergo the following treatment:
DIET - STRICTLY FORBIDDEN:
All acoholic beverages (wine, beer, cider, spirits, cocktails,
Good-day, gentlemen! I hope I'm not intruding?
No? Well, I'm happy to tell you my machine is ready now. When may I come aboard?
You can't come aboard! We aren't interested in your machine!
Tomorrow?
No not tomorrow! Never!
Today? . . . Good. I'll go and fetch it at once.

Blistering barnacles! You may be deaf, but you aren't blind, are you?

WE ARE NOT INTERESTED IN YOUR MACHINE!

That's that! Now he understands!

Let's hope so.

Captain, is what Tintin says really true? He's just told us you've decided not to go. It seems you broke a mirror and are afraid . . .

Afraid?

Me, afraid? . . . Afraid of what? . . . Afraid of whom? . . . Afraid of you, perhaps? Captain Haddock fears nothing! You understand? We weigh anchor at dawn tomorrow, no matter what anyone says! . . .

OUCH! . . .

At last we are on our way, Snowy.

Tintin!

A radio message . . .

"Port Commander to Captain SIRIUS. Reduce speed. Motor boat coming out to you." What can this mean?

Look! . . . There's a motor boat coming now.

I can't quite see the passenger; but it'd better not be Professor Calculus!

Thomson and Thompson! What are they coming aboard for?

Hello! We're coming with you!

Coming with us? . . .

Yes, we've had orders to protect you.

Protect us? Is someone threatening us? . . .

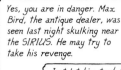
Yes, you are in danger. Max Bird, the antique dealer, was seen last night skulking near the SIRIUS. He may try to take his revenge.

Just let him try! He'll find out . . .

Maybe, maybe. But anyway, now we are aboard you will be able to feel that you are perfectly safe.

To be precise: perfectly safe.

We shall see . . . Meanwhile we must find you a berth. Let's see . . . We've a couple of spare bunks for'ard. Will that do?

Yes, thanks!

Captain! . . . Captain!

Captain, I can't stand it!

What?

This thieving Snowy - he's stolen a whole box of biscuits!

No? . . .

Snowy? . . .

Yes, Snowy! I saw him just now near the galley!

Snowy! . . . Where is the wretched animal?

Snowy? . . . SNOWY? . . .

I can't see him, the scoundrel! But don't worry, I'll see that it doesn't happen again . . .

Good.

Er . . . our cabin is for'ard, isn't it?

Yes, for'ard.

We'll change at once, and mix discreetly with the ship's company . . .

Good idea!

We must behave like old sea-dogs . . .

For a start, we'd better learn to chew tobacco. All old sea-dogs chew a quid. Here, have one of these . . .

What do we do, Captain? We're bearing down on that fishing fleet . . .

Give a blast on the siren; that'll warn them.

TOOOOOT

Goodness! . . . My tobacco! . . .

Mine . . . mine too . . . I swallowed it! . . .

Next day . . .

This has got to stop! . . . Yes, it's got to stop!

Yes, Captain. Yesterday it was a box of biscuits! This morning a whole chicken has disappeared!

The wretched dog!

Snowy! . . . Snowy! . . . Where's he hiding? . . . Snowy!

Snowy! . . . Snowy! . . .

Snowy! . . . Snowy! . . . Where on earth can he be hiding? . . .

You really saw him make off with the chicken?

Well, I didn't exactly see him, but I supposed . . .

You supposed! . . . You supposed! . . . Don't you accuse anyone of anything unless you have proof! . . . Besides, how do we know you didn't eat the chicken yourself? . . .

That evening . . .

Good night. You might just keep an eye on Snowy.

Don't worry. I'll watch him! Good night Captain . . .

THIEF!

SAME TO YOU . . .

Crumbs! That's the two detectives . . .

What's going on here? . . .

! !

It's him, Tintin! . . . He's stolen my pillow!

That's not true! It's him – he's taken one of my blankets!

Aren't you ashamed, at your age? Quarrelling over such trifles! Now, that's all over, isn't it?

Now let's go to bed!

Billions of blistering barnacles!

?

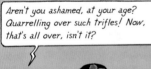

What's the matter, Captain?

The matter? Blistering barnacles, my bottle of whisky has vanished!

Vanished? Someone must be worried about your health and is keeping you to your diet . . .

You can laugh! . . . But if I catch the crook, he's in for a rough time!

We'll investigate it in the morning. Now let's go to bed. I'm dead tired. Good night!

You go to sleep if you like. I know what I'm going to do.

NO

NO ENTRY

OLD SCOTCH WHISKY

Thundering typhoons!

OLD SCOTCH WHISKY

NO ENTRY

THUMP THUMP THUMP

Tintin, Tintin, come quickly! . . . There's not a moment to lose!

We're going to blow up! . . . There's a bomb in the hold! . . .

I went down to the hold to open a case of whisky. And instead of whisky I found a bomb there! . . .

Here we are . . . Careful!

In here . . . Look . . .

NO ENTRY

Careful! . . . Don't go near it!

I must. We've got to get to the bottom of this . . .

Well? . . .

Steel plates!

Steel plates? . . .

NO ENTRY

You're right, by thunder! . . . Then it's not a bomb after all? . . .

Definitely not. Look, we'll open another case . . .

Blistering barnacles! More steel plates!

And in this one . . .

More steel plates!

Steaming blood! There's not a drop of whisky aboard! If I catch the monster who played this trick on us, he'll be in for a rough time! . . .

Come on, Captain. We'll try and solve this mystery in the morning . . .

Next day . . .

Anyway, we can't accuse Snowy any more. Some biscuits, even a chicken perhaps. But not a bottle of whisky!

OH!

Great snakes! . . . He . . . he . . . why, he's drunk!

Snowy, what have you done? Pooh! Your breath smells of whisky!

Now come on! . . . Show us where you found the whisky . . .

All right . . . You . . . you want a d-d-d-drink too?

? ?

Look!

See, the bottle must have smashed up there. Let's investigate.

There!

Blistering barnacles! If I ever catch him!

Sh! . . . Listen . . .

ZZZ . . . ZZZ . . . ZZZ . . .

Someone is asleep in this life-boat!

Impossible: the lashings are secure . . . At least . . .

Blistering barnacles! The lashings are free this side! There's someone in this life-boat!

! *Thundering typhoons!*

ZZZ... ZZZ... ZZZ...

Billions of bilious blue blistering barnacles! Get up, you!...

My whisky, you wretch!... What have you done with my whisky? Thundering typhoons, answer me!... Where's my whisky?

I must confess, I did sleep rather badly. But I hope you will give me a cabin...

A cabin!... I'll give you a cabin!... I'm going to stow you in the bottom of the hold for the rest of the voyage, on dry bread and water!... And my whisky?... Where's my whisky?

It's on board, of course!

It's on board!... Heaven be praised!

Naturally it is in separate pieces...

In separate pieces... My whisky is in separate pieces?

Of course, it is a little smaller than the first one, but nevertheless it was too big to pass unnoticed. So I had to dismantle it and pack all the parts in the cases...

But what about the whisky out of those cases! Tell me! Is it still ashore?...

Oh no!

No, no. It was night before you sailed. The cases were still on the quay, ready to be embarked. I took out all the bottles they contained, and put the pieces of my machine in their place...

Wretch!... Ignoramus!... Abominable Snowman!... I'll throw you overboard! Overboard, d'you hear?...

Thank you, Captain, thank you very much! It's just what I expected from you... Such a kind welcome! You'll see - you won't regret it.

Some days later...

SIRIUS

Look. We have reached the position indicated by the parchments. We should soon see the island off which the *UNICORN* sank...

Isn't the island marked on any charts?

No, but that sometimes happens with small, unimportant islands. Come on, we'll try to spot it...

I can't see anything yet... Can you?...

Nothing.

Can you see anything?...

Not yet. But there's a bottle of champagne for the first one to sight land!

Over there!

Where's the island?... I can't see anything...

It was, Captain. A shark, I know it was! I saw one, I really did!

Still no sign . . . It's very strange . . .

What's the name of the island?

How should I know? . . . It's not marked on any of the charts.

Oh? . . . But you are sure we're near it?

Positive! I plotted the position yesterday at noon.

Yes, I see. But . . . er . . . supposing you made a mistake in your calculations . . .

!

Oh, so I made a mistake in my calculations, did I? . . . All right: they're on my table. Go and check them! . . . Yes, you! Now! Go on! Check them!

Tell me, Captain, was that a fish jumping out of the water just now?

No, it was a grand piano!

Ah, I didn't think it could have been a fish . . .

A few minutes later . . .

You must forgive me, Captain, but there really is a little mistake in your calculations. Look, this is where we are exactly . . .

You are right . . . I have made a mistake. Gentlemen, please take off your hats . . .

Why must we take off our hats, Captain? . . .

Sh! . . .

? ?

Now . . .

But Captain, tell us what you mean . . .

24

I mean, gentlemen, that according to your calculations we are now standing inside Westminster Abbey!

Thousands of thundering typhoons! Where's that miserable island got to?

I'm beginning to think Sir Francis Haddock was pulling our legs.

I'm beginning to think so too!

We'll soon see! It's almost noon. We'll take a sight. I'll go and fetch my sextant.

That's it . . . Let's go in, and I'll work it out . . .

The figures given in the parchments were latitude 20°37'42" North, longitude 70°52'15" West. Here's our position now; the same latitude, longitude 71°2'29" West.

So we've already passed the right point, and yet we saw nothing . . . I simply can't understand it!

Captain, I think I've got it!

!

What do you mean?

Well, the meridian from which you calculated the degrees of longitude was of course the Greenwich meridian . . .

You don't suppose I used one in Timbuctoo!

No, wait. Supposing Sir Francis Haddock used a French chart - he easily could have done. Then zero would be on the Paris meridian - and that lies more than two degrees east of Greenwich!

Blistering barnacles, that's an idea! You may be right! Perhaps we are too far to the west. We'll go back on our tracks . . .

Coxswain at the wheel! ... Helm hard a-port! ... Midships! ... Steer due east.

?

Captain, what is happening? ... We seem to be turning back.

Yes, Professor Calculus, we're turning back.

Oh, that's all right then ... I was afraid we were turning back.

How easy it is to be mistaken. I'd have sworn we'd turned back.

That evening ...

There it is at last! Our treasure island!

It's too late to go ashore tonight. We'll drop anchor, and tomorrow we'll explore the island ...

Right! ...

Next morning ...

Haul the boat up the beach. I'm going to reconnoitre.

BANG

Crumbs! What's happened to him?

Captain, what was it? Are you hurt?

No. I stubbed my toe against that thing and fell over. That's how the gun went off . . .

OW! OW!

Keep calm! Keep calm!

YOW!

Here . . .

YEOW!

YOW!

YEOW!

Oh, leave them . . . Come and help me dig up this piece of wood. It intrigues me.

Hello, what have they found?

These are the remains of the jolly boat in which Sir Francis Haddock once came ashore on this island . . .

This certainly proves that we're nearing our goal. Red Rackham's treasure is out there at the bottom of the sea! . . . But now, shoes on, everyone, and let's carry on!

WOOAH!

That's Snowy! . . . He ran on ahead! . . .

? !

Where did you get that bone from Snowy? . . . Here, show us where you found it.

Blistering barnacles! I bet these are the remains of the pirates killed when the *UNICORN* blew up!

They can't be, Captain.

If they were, we'd have found them down by the shore. No, look at this spear. It's more likely that they were natives, killed in a fight, and probably eaten on the spot by their enemies.

Eaten? . . . Do you mean cannibals lived on this island? . . . Man-eaters?

That's what we're going to find out. Come on.

Ouch! I've got a pebble in my shoe!

You go on. I'll catch you up . . .

Look! . . . There! . . .

An idol! . . .

Yes, an idol . . . But . . . It's incredible.

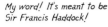

My word! It's meant to be Sir Francis Haddock!

Look at that mouth! His voice must have made an enormous impression on the natives. I can just imagine their faces the first time they heard him shout: "Ration my rum!"

RRRATION MY RRRUM!

What's the matter, Captain?

Who shouted like that?

What? . . . Wasn't it you?

No, it wasn't me! Thundering typhoons!

Yes, it's Sir Francis Haddock.

RRRATION MY RRRUM!

It came from over there.

Not a soul!

This island is h-h-haunted, Captain. Let's hurry back t-t-to the sh-sh-ship.

To b-b-be precise: I-let's hurry back t-t-to the sh-sh-ship.

Pithecanthropus! . . . Pockmark! . . .

Pockmark yourself, you gibbering ghost!

Come out if you dare, Polynesian!
... Cannibal! ... Iconoclast! ...

Nincompoop! ...
Ruffian! ...
Baboon!

Up there! ...

Baboon!

Squawking popinjay!

Sea-gherkin!

Pickled herring!

Blistering barnacles!
Parrots!!

Yes, parrots! From
generation to generation
your ancestor's vocabulary
has been handed down!

Pockmark! ...
Freshwater
swabs! ...
Bully! ...

Me, a bully?
You called
me a bully
did you? ...

I'll show you
what I'm
made of!

Here's a coconut to cut your
cackle, iconoclasts!!!

Ooh, my
back!

Wait, I'll rub it
for you.

Your gun! ... Give me your
gun! ... I'm going to turn them
into parrot soup.

Hey, Captain, calm yourself. After all, they're only parrots!

Bandits!

Forget about them, Captain. Let's go on.

You're right. Come on, let's go.

My gun! . . . Who has taken my gun? . . .

I only left it there for a moment . . .

Perhaps it fell into the bush?

Got it?

No . . . It's vanished completely!

Blue blistering . . .

Sh! . . . Listen!

What's that noise?

Crooee! . . . Crooee! . . . Crooee! . . .

Crooee! . . . Crooee! . . .

Blistering baboons! . . . Monkeys! . . . Gibbons! . . . Orang-outangs! . . . Give us back that gun, cercopithecuses!

That's no use, Captain. Leave it to me. I'll frighten them.

Hands up! . . . Bang! . . . Bang! . . . Bang!

Hey, don't do that!

BANG

!

That's done it! . . . They've dropped the gun! . . . Look, here it comes . . .

Very smart, weren't you, eh? . . . Look! . . . Another inch lower, and that would have been the end of Captain Haddock!

Anyway, all's well that ends well! . . . Shall we go back now, Captain? . . . We know the island is uninhabited.

Good idea. Let's go.

Thundering typhoons! I just remembered!

The idol! . . . Are we going to leave it here?

Ah! What pleasant visions haunt me
As I gaze upon the sea!
All the old romantic legends.
All my dreams, come back to me . . .

Look out! . . . A shark! . . .

Thundering typhoons! . . . It almost had my hand off!

Look there's another! . . . And there . . . and there . . .

Quick, the gun! I'll tell them a thing or two, the brutes!

BING

You know, Captain, I'm beginning to think Professor Calculus's machine may come in very handy for us . . .

Next day . . .

You've made up your mind?

Yes . . . Professor Calculus has explained exactly how his machine works. It'll be all right . . .

Stop! . . . Just a minute! . . .

I forgot to tell you. When you locate the wreck, press the little red button on the left of the instrument panel. That releases a small canister attached underneath the machine. It is full of a substance that gives off thick smoke when it comes into contact with water. That will show us where the wreck lies.

A little red button? . . . Right!

No, red! A little red button . . . You've got it? Good . . . Well, goodbye, and good luck!

There he goes: he's dived.

This is fun, eh Snowy?

Golly, what a lot of water!

Let's hope nothing goes wrong . . .

Gone long? Why, it's only ten minutes since he dived . . .

Hello, what's the matter? . . .
The engine's stopped . . .
We aren't moving any more!

?!

Thing's look bad, Snowy!
Our propeller is entangled
in the weeds!

We'll try and free ourselves by going
into reverse . . .

It's no good! The propeller
is completely jammed . . .
and the engine has stalled!

Well, Snowy my boy, how do we
get out of this?

There's only one thing
to do: we'll release the
smoke-canister. Then
at least they'll know
where we are . . .
There, we press the
little red button here . . .

That's it . . .

Look! . . . Look! . . . Smoke! . . . He's
found the wreck of the UNICORN!

There, Professor Calculus! . . .
Look! . . . Smoke! . . . He's
found the wreck!

OH!

Captain, look there! . . . Look! . . . No, over there! Smoke! . . . He's found the wreck!

Patience, Snowy! . . . It won't be long before someone comes to rescue us.

Ahoy there! . . . Lower the dinghy! . . . We'll drop a buoy over the spot Tintin has marked.

There's the buoy . . .

. . . And there's the underwater viewing instrument.

It worries me a bit that Tintin hasn't come up again . . .

No, but I was a great sportsman in my youth . . .

. . . And that accounts for the athletic figure I still have . . .

Hm? . . .

To be quite honest, no . . . It was mostly walking . . .

Let's see . . .

Thundering typhoons! . . . It's not the wreck! . . . It's Tintin!

Wonderful! Quick, let me look . . .

Oh, Columbus! . . . The propeller has been fouled by weeds! . . . How can we save him?

 Really, Captain! Your eyes have deceived you! It's not the wreck, it is Tintin. He can't resurface . . .

 Your confounded contraption! I should never have let him go down!

May drown? Well, he had enough oxygen for two hours. He's got . . . Let's see . . . yes, he has just enough for another ten minutes!

 I hope they hurry! It's getting more and more difficult to breathe . . .

 What can we do? How can we save him?

Lower a diver? . . . No, by the time we'd got one equipped and ready, Tintin would be dead . . .

 No, I've go an idea. Take the anchor! . . . The anchor used for mooring the buoy!

The anchor? What for? . . .

 Of course! . . . We'll try and hook it on to the submarine. Then we'll pull on the rope until the weeds break . . .

 That's it! Let it down . . . Lower . . . lower . . . lower . . . gently . . .

 An anchor! . . . They're going to try to hook me. Quick, empty the ballast tanks, that'll help them . . .

 He's understood. He's emptied the ballast tanks to lighten the submarine . . . A bit to the left, Captain . . . Good . . . Now, pull!

 Ah, they've got it! . . . I'm saved! . . . Just in time! I'm suffocating.

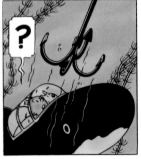 ?

 Missed! . . . The anchor hadn't caught properly. Lower it again . . . down . . . stop! A bit to the right . . . now to the left . . . Pull it up gently . . .

Pull! . . . Pull! . . . For goodness' sake pull!

Pull! . . . Go on, pull!

Thundering typhoons, I'm trying to! What do you think I'm doing? Playing the cornet?

Billions of blue blistering barnacles! I hope there aren't any sharks about.

Fresh air! . . . Fresh air at last! . . .

Hooray! . . . He's safe! . . . Hip-hip-hooray!

All's well! . . . The Captain has climbed back into the boat . . . He's salvaged the buoy . . . hauled the anchor inboard . . . thrown a lifeline to Tintin . . . Ah, here they come . . .

Well, our friend Tintin had a narrow escape!

You are wrong, I assure you. Weeds jammed the propeller. You'll see when we're back on board.

You see? . . . It's just as I said. Weeds . . .

Really? I thought they were weeds . . .

Weeds or no weeds, I don't set foot in that thing again! . . .

Fine. Get it ready. Snowy and I are setting out again immediately!

Let's hope he doesn't run into any more trouble this time . . .

What shall I do? Tell him . . . or not?

I've made up my mind . . .

I . . . Captain . . . I've bad news for you.

Bad news for me?

No, bad news for you, very bad news . . . I'm afraid the UNICORN is not here . . . Look . . .

What's that gadget, eh?

40

Yes, it's a pendulum. I've taken up the study of divining, and I've arrived at the conclusion I just gave you . . .

All from that whatsit?

Yes, much further west . . . You'll see. My pendulum will begin swinging from east to west . . . Look, it's started . . .

You see? . . . It's swinging westwards. The UNICORN will be found in that direction.

Look there, Captain! Smoke!

And look, there's the submarine surfacing! . . . This time we've got it! . . . He's found the wreck!

Have you found it?

Westwards . . . It's still westwards.

Yes. I've found the UNICORN! . . . You can prepare the diving equipment!

You're sure you'll be all right? . . .

Certain! I'll do everything exactly as you told me . . .

Good! Now, don't forget . . . If you want to come up, jerk the line twice . . . In an emergency, give a series of quick jerks.

Right!

Come on, pump hard!

We are!

?

Wooah! Wooah!

Wooah! Wooah!

That's it, he's touched bottom . . .

So this is the UNICORN!

Crumbs! What's happening? The air supply has stopped! . . .

Thundering typhoons! What are you two doing there, instead of pumping?

Us? We're resting . . . it's tiring work, you know.

You infernal impersonations of abominable snowmen! Pump for your lives! . . . Faster!

Whew! . . . That's better! . . . Now the air's coming again. That gave me quite a fright . . .

Excuse me, Captain, but I don't understand . . . Since the UNICORN is not here, why has Tintin gone down?

He's picking daisies down below!

?

Having a row? I don't see a boat?

Two jerks on the line! He wants to come up. I'm sure he must have found something!

Heave-ho! . . . Heave-ho!

Here he is.

What has he got?

A gold cross, encrusted with precious stones! . . . and a cutlass! . . . I say, this cross is superb!

We've made a good start, eh?

Now why did he tell me that Tintin had gone for a row?

Yes, it's a good start. But this is nothing to what else we shall find. You'll see. I'm going down myself, this time.

By the way . . . er . . . any sign of sharks?

No, none at all.

Here's your helmet.

Good.

Ow! . . . OOH! . . . OW!

Whatever's the matter?

Blistering barnacles! My beard!

!

There, now your beard is inside.

Good. You can close my helmet now. Keep an eye on that pumping.

Aha! Now to find the treasure! . . .

A few minutes later . . .

A series of jerks! . . . The danger signal! . . .

Hurry! Hurry! Pull him up! . . . Something frightful must have happened!

Let's hope that it's not a shark . . .

At last!

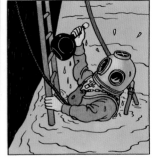

A bottle? What can that mean? . . .

A bottle of rum, my friends! . . . Jamaica rum, and it's more than two hundred and fifty years old! . . . Just you taste it!

GLUG GLUG GLUG GLUG

GLUG GLUG GLUG

Mm! . . . It's wonderful! . . . It's absolutely w-w-wonderful! Y-y-you taste it! . . . Yes, yes, that's f-f-for you! . . . I'm g-g-going st-st-st-straight back to g-get a-a-a another f-for m-myself . . .

That beats everything! He's gone in without his helmet!

Billions of bilious blue blistering barnacles! Those two jelly-fishes forgot to pump again! . . .

Sea-gherkins! . . . Freshwater swabs! . . . Ectoplasms! . . . Bashi-bazouks! . . .

But . . . but it wasn't us, you . . .

Silence! You were told to pump, then pump, by thunder!

It's no use drying yourself, Captain. You must empty your suit first . . . Take it off now.

Take it off? . . . Never! . . . Never! . . .

I'll rest a minute and go down again . . .

You see? ... I told you so! ... Your suit is full of water ... We'll have to empty it.

There! Now you can go down again, if you still want to. But don't forget your helmet this time!

Off we go! ... As for you, my hearties, just you keep on pumping until you're ordered to stop! ... You understand? ...

Yes, yes, we're pumping ...

There he goes now ...

The same evening ...

A good day's work! ... First that cross, and then ... more important, all this rum! ... Fine stuff eh?

Yes, but I'd sooner have found the treasure.

Oh, we'll find that tomorrow, won't we Professor Calculus? ...

Perhaps, but I'm inclined to think it is rum.

CHEEEP CHEEEP CHEEEP

Ssh!

It sounds like a bird ...

I'd say it was the squeak of a badly greased wheel ...

CHEEEP

Let's see. I want to set my mind at rest.

There, Captain. It's the pump making that noise.

46

CHEEEP
CHEEEP

What d'you think you're doing at this hour?

You never ordered us to stop pumping, Captain. So here we are, pumping.

To be precise: we're pumping.

Off to bed, nitwits! You'll have plenty more pumping, believe me!

The next morning . . .

Something tells me Tintin is going to find the treasure this morning.

Another bottle of rum! . . . I'll leave it there for the Captain.

Hello, I wonder what we've got here?

A casket! Great snakes! Can it be Red Rackham's treasure?

I'll go straight up, and see what's inside this casket!

He's grabbed the casket!

Goodness, he's swallowed it! And he's coming back for me!

He's coming again. What can I do? If only I had a weapon.

Perhaps this bottle will help . . .

Quick, back against this old rib. Then he won't sever my air-pipe . . .

Good heavens,
what a blow!

Thank goodness my
suit isn't damaged.

?

My stars!
He's drunk!

Now he's sleeping it off, I suppose.
Here's my chance to try and recover
the casket.

Two jerks on
the line! He
wants us to
pull him up.

Heave-ho! Heave-ho! . . .
You wait! He'll be
bringing us the
treasure.

Thundering
typhoons! Why
does he have
to struggle so?

?

Blistering barnacles, a
shark! What a fellow;
he's caught a shark!
. . . But what does he
want us to do with it?

The best thing is to ask him.

Of course! . . . Lower
another line to him, and pull
him up.

Now, up I go.
I wonder
what the
Captain
will say!

49

Well, what's the meaning of this little joke?

Little joke? . . . Just cut open that shark, Captain, and you'll see.

In any case, I believe the fins are particularly tasty . . .

a few minutes later . . .

Captain! . . . Captain! . . . Look what we found in the shark's stomach!

A casket! . . . A casket! . . . Red Rackham's treasure! Red Rackham's treasure!! . . . Here it is at last!

Quick, into my cabin!

Hm! . . . Not so easy! It's all rusted up.

It's no good, you'll snap the blade. Better try this case opener.

Good idea. Hold it tight, you two.

Go on! Go on: don't worry, we're holding it . . .

CRACK

Got it! . . .

Billions of bilious blue blistering barnacles in a thundering typhoon! . . . It's not the treasure!

These are old documents, half eaten away by damp!

Documents? Fine! And what am I supposed to do with documents?

Come now, Captain, don't lose heart! . . . We'll continue our search.

What's the use?

That's it! . . . I've got it!

These are old documents! . . . Definitely! . . . Old documents!

That chap will drive me crazy!

And you there? Thundering typhoons, what are you doing?

Me? . . . You can see - I'm helping my colleague to go down . . . Oh, don't worry. I've watched carefully how you do it . . .

What about the pump? The pump works by itself, I suppose?

I'll work the pump, nincompoop! . . . Then at least I'll know he's safe.

Thundering typhoons! What's that over there, on the deck?

The weighted boots! . . . He's forgotten the weighted boots!

A fortnight later . . .
Here we are, pumping as usual . . . As usual . . .

Blistering barnacles! You can stop pumping! Can't you see that Tintin's come up?

Well?
Nothing . . . Nothing at all! I've been carefully through all that's left of the poop . . .

It's just as I said: we aren't going to find it.
Come on, Captain, you . . .

51

Tell me, what is that cross over there?

A cross? Where can you see a cross?

No, a cross . . . that cross over there on the island.

It certainly is a cross, isn't it? . . .

I say, Captain, Professor Calculus is right! There is a cross, over on the tip of the island!

A cross?

You think so?

Thundering typhoons! It is indeed a cross!

Really? I'd have sworn it was a cross!

Hooray! . . . Hip-hip-hip-hoo-ray! . . . I've got it!

?

Professor Calculus, Professor Calculus, you've saved us!

Let me waltz ♪♪ with you ♫ , The whole ♪♪ night through ♫♫

Quickly, Captain! . . . Picks! . . . Shovels! . . . We're going back to the island.

Yes, Captain, the treasure lies there! You remember the words in Sir Francis Haddock's message: "then shines forth the Eagle's cross". There it is: the Eagle's cross!

Thundering typhoons! You're right!

Hooray! Thomson! . . . Thompson! . . . Fetch the picks and shovels! Hurry up! . . . Into the dinghy!

Well, Professor Calculus, we can never thank you enough!

It is rather rough . . .

No, I said it is thanks to you that we are going to find the treasure.

Oh . . . Well, I'm sure it's a cross!

Of course, of course it is a cross . . .

No? . . . D'you think so?

Baboon! Freshwater swab!

Hello, my old friend!

Hooray! Here it is!

Gentlemen, this is it, the Eagle's cross!

Well, what did I tell you? Is it or is it not a cross?

Why, what's the meaning of all these notches?

A calendar! When your ancestor was marooned – like Robinson Crusoe, he counted the days until he was rescued. Look: there's a small notch for weekdays, and a large one for Sundays . . .

To work, to work! I'll give a bottle of rum to whoever finds the treasure!

Are you . . . er . . . looking for something? . . .

!

Blistering barnacles, put away your pendulum; come and give us a hand instead!

Towards the west; yes, it does . . .

What can they be searching for like that?

But . . . no, it's impossible!

What? . . . What is so impossible?

That the treasure can be here!

W-w-what? . . . Why? . . .

Just think . . . Supposing Sir Francis Haddock left the UNICORN, carrying the treasure; why would he have buried it here, at the foot of this cross? . . . What would you have done in his place? On the day you left this island you'd have taken the treasure with you, wouldn't you?

But then . . .

Then? . . . Probably the treasure is still out there, under the sea! . . . And we've followed a false trail!

All because of that creature Calculus, blistering barnacles!

Yes, it's all your fault, you certified ignoramus!

Yes; I'm tired of telling you: it's further westwards!

Westwards! . . . Westwards! . . . I'll give you westwards!

OH!

Now your infernal pendulum's gone west, you Olympic athlete, you!

Wooah! Wooah!

Take that! . . . And that! . . . Now it's buried, pestilential pendulum!

There! . . . And don't mention it again! Come on now, we're going back!

He's furious!

What a good little doggie you are! . . .

Down, Snowy! ...No more games, now!

Is something bothering the Captain?. . . He seems to be rather worried!

Where have the Siamese twins got to?

Why, I thought they were behind us.

AHOY! THOMSON! THOMPSON!

No, no, please don't worry. The little dog brought it back for me.

Billions of blue blistering barnacles! This time I've had enough!

Captain! Captain!

Leave me alone! I've got to let fly at something!

Thousands of thundering typhoons! That's the lot, eh?

55

Now, Captain, you sit down while I go and have a look for those two...

All right.

I wonder where they've got to, the sillies!

Where has Tintin gone?

He's gone west!

I think I can hear them.

What on earth are you doing here?

Us?... We're filling in this hole... It's safer... People never look where they're going...

Next day...

Well, you've quite made up your mind to go on searching?

For a few more days, Captain. Look, today is the 9th. If we haven't found anything by the 15th, we'll give up the game and go home...

Just as you please...

You won't regret it. And it will give us a chance to try and raise some of the remains of the UNICORN... The figurehead, for instance.

Off we go! Pumping again!

Here's to the 15th when we'll be able to stop! I'm fed up with this business...

Come to think of it, I haven't seen Calculus today. Is he ill?

10
THURSDAY

11
FRIDAY

What's up with Calculus? He's not left his cabin for three days.

12
SATURDAY

13
SUNDAY
Still no luck, Captain . . .

14
MONDAY

15
TUESDAY

?

What . . . What's happening? . . . It looks as if . . .

Oh dear, I'm right! . . . I must warn the Captain!

Come on, Captain, don't let this upset you. It's bad luck, I know, but you must make the best of it . . .

Captain! . . . Captain! . . . The ship is sailing!

Well, what would you like it to do? Dance a jig?

Ah, I see now. At last you have realised that the UNICORN is not where you were looking; you are steering westwards. I understand . . .

I've had enough! Come with me!

You see that, eh? I suppose it's the figure-head of the TITANIC!

My word, it's a unicorn! But what about my pendulum, which swung to the west? . . . How extraordinary . . .

16
WEDNESDAY
17
THURSDAY
18
FRIDAY
19
SATURDAY
20
SUNDAY
21
MONDAY
22
TUESDAY

RRRING
RRRING

JULY
23

Hello. Yes . . . "Daily Reporter" . . . Yes . . . What? The SIRIUS has docked? . . . Are you sure? . . . Good . . . Thanks!

Hello, is that you Rogers? . . . Go to the docks at once. The SIRIUS has just come in . . . I want a good story about her!

Well, Captain, I'll say goodbye to you now. I'll have my submarine collected tomorrow morning.

All right. Good.

Now, please let me thank you, Captain. You have been so very kind.

Oh, it was nothing.

Yes, yes, Captain. Thanks to you. I shall always have unforgettable memories of my stay on board . . .

So shall I!

THUD

Er . . . excuse me . . . I missed a step!

Allow me to introduce myself: Ken Rogers of the "Daily Reporter".

"Daily Reporter"? Wasn't yours the paper that gave the news of our departure?

It was! . . . And we would like to publish a sensational article about your trip. May I ask you a few questions?

Of course . . .

I'm rather busy myself. This is my secretary, Mr Calculus; he will be happy to answer all your inquiries.

Delighted . . .

Now Mr Calculus, about the treasure . . . . Oh . . . yes.

I'm sure you have it there, in the suitcase . . .

Thank you, I'll carry it myself.

I can understand that! . . . Now tell me, what does the treasure consist of?

No? . . . Not really? . . .

No, I asked you what was in the treasure you found. Was it gold? . . . Pearls? . . . Diamonds?

Incredible! I don't believe a word of it!

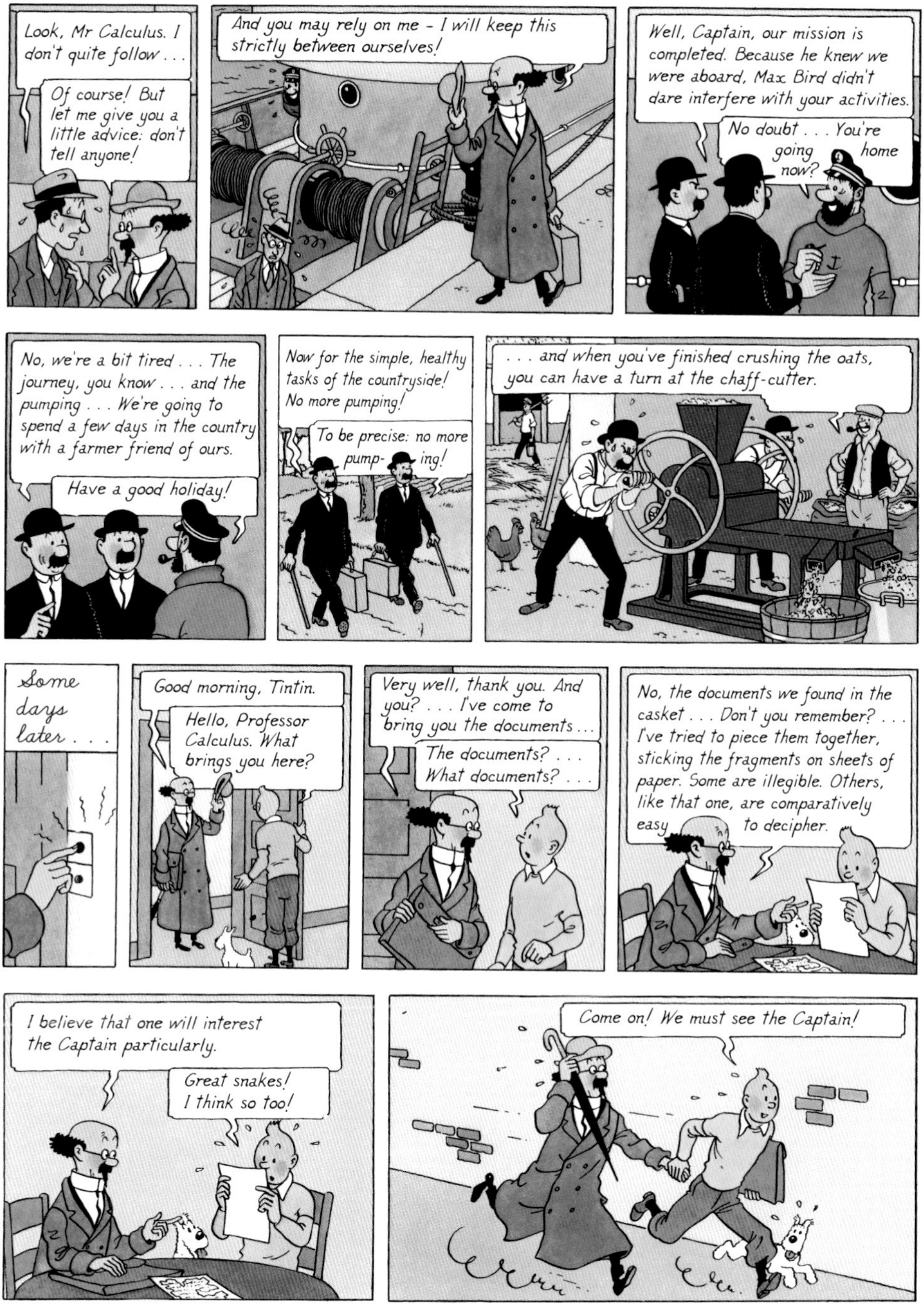
Look, Mr Calculus. I don't quite follow . . .
Of course! But let me give you a little advice: don't tell anyone!
And you may rely on me - I will keep this strictly between ourselves!
Well, Captain, our mission is completed. Because he knew we were aboard, Max Bird didn't dare interfere with your activities.
No doubt . . . You're going home now?
No, we're a bit tired . . . The journey, you know . . . and the pumping . . . We're going to spend a few days in the country with a farmer friend of ours.
Have a good holiday!
Now for the simple, healthy tasks of the countryside! No more pumping!
To be precise: no more pump- ing!
. . . and when you've finished crushing the oats, you can have a turn at the chaff-cutter.
Some days later . . .
Good morning, Tintin.
Hello, Professor Calculus. What brings you here?
Very well, thank you. And you? . . . I've come to bring you the documents . . .
The documents? . . . What documents? . . .
No, the documents we found in the casket . . . Don't you remember? . . . I've tried to piece them together, sticking the fragments on sheets of paper. Some are illegible. Others, like that one, are comparatively easy to decipher.
I believe that one will interest the Captain particularly.
Great snakes! I think so too!
Come on! We must see the Captain!

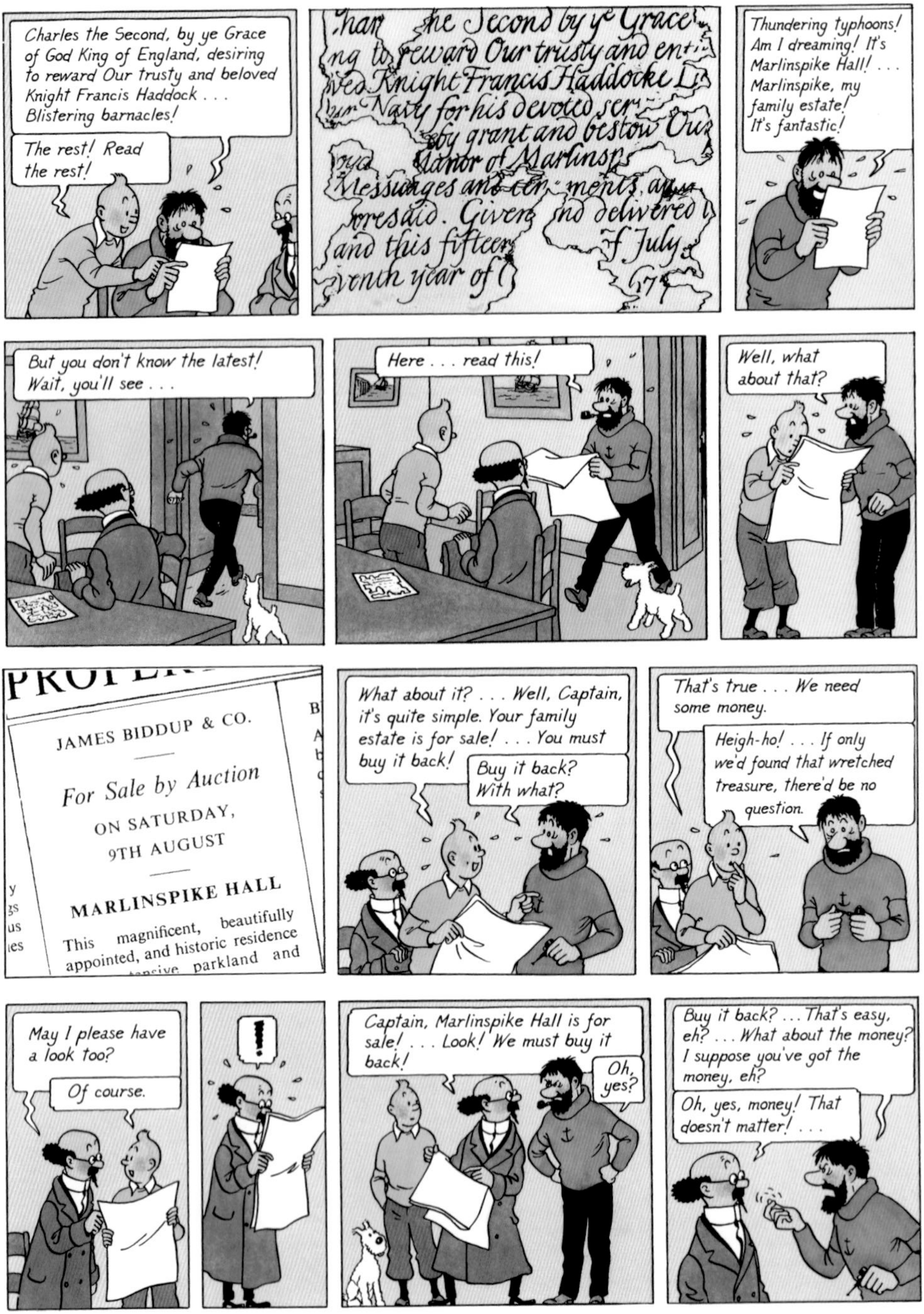
Charles the Second, by ye Grace of God King of England, desiring to reward Our trusty and beloved Knight Francis Haddock . . . Blistering barnacles!
The rest! Read the rest!
Thundering typhoons! Am I dreaming! It's Marlinspike Hall! . . . Marlinspike, my family estate! It's fantastic!
But you don't know the latest! Wait, you'll see . . .
Here . . . read this!
Well, what about that?
JAMES BIDDUP & CO.
For Sale by Auction
ON SATURDAY, 9TH AUGUST
MARLINSPIKE HALL
This magnificent, beautifully appointed, and historic residence
parkland and
What about it? . . . Well, Captain, it's quite simple. Your family estate is for sale! . . . You must buy it back!
Buy it back? With what?
That's true . . . We need some money.
Heigh-ho! . . . If only we'd found that wretched treasure, there'd be no question.
May I please have a look too?
Of course.
!
Captain, Marlinspike Hall is for sale! . . . Look! We must buy it back!
Oh, yes?
Buy it back? . . . That's easy, eh? . . . What about the money? I suppose you've got the money, eh?
Oh, yes, money! That doesn't matter! . . .

That's all right! I have some money.

You? . . . You've got money? . . . That's nice for you! . . . Personally, I haven't any!

Quite! The government have paid me a large sum for the patent on my submarine. Thanks to you I was able to try it out. Now it's my turn to help you . . . Come along, we're going to buy your mansion.

HOUSE FOR SALE

HOUSE is not FOR SALE

All's well that ends well! . . . You haven't found the treasure, but you have got back your family estate.

It is magnificent!

Wait, you haven't seen anything yet.

This is the room where I telephoned you.

Splendid!

SSH!

No . . . Nothing . . . I thought I heard footsteps . . .

Oh?

Well, it's a wonderful house! . . . My ancestor had good taste, didn't he? . . . Now what about those famous cellars you talked of? Where are they?

Come with me . . . I'll take you there.

Look! Here we are!

Thundering typhoons!

What a lot of junk! . . . All this junk!

Oh yes, the Bird brothers used this as a storeroom.

Look, that's St. John the Evangelist. We must be in an old chapel . . .

What do you think of it?

Incre-   dible!

Sh! . . . This time I'm sure I heard a noise!

It's gone . . . The footsteps have stopped . . . It's queer. I wonder . . .

What?

Why, whatever's the matter? What is it?

Hooray!

The Eagle's cross! . . . "And then shines forth the Eagle's cross"! There it is . . . the Eagle's cross . . .

The Eagle's cross? . . . I can see a cross, but where is the Eagle?

There, in front of you!

Yes there, look! . . . St. John the Evangelist - who is always depicted with an eagle . . . And he's called the Eagle of Patmos - after the island where he wrote his Revelation . . . He's the Eagle! . . .

There's a globe!

And an eagle! . . . You're right! . . .

There, just on the spot given in the old parchment, is the island we went to! . . . Great snakes! The island's moving!

The treasure! . . . The treasure!! . . . Blistering treasures! It's Red Rackham's barnacles!

We've found it! . . . We've found it at last: Red Rackham's treasure! . . . Look! . . . Look!

It's stupendous! . . . Stupendous! . . . So Sir Francis Haddock did take the treasure with him when he left the UNICORN . . . And to think we were looking for it half across the world, when all the time it was lying here, right under our very noses . . .

Thundering typhoons, look at this! . . . Diamonds! . . . Pearls! . . . Emeralds! . . . Rubies! . . . Er . . . all sorts! . . . They're magnificent!

Sh! . . . Did you hear that?

Yes . . .

Listen . . . Footsteps! . . . Someone's coming towards the cellars . . .

Quick! Get hold of a weapon! We'll each hide behind a pillar . . .

Right! Come on!

CAPTAIN HADDOCK
Requests the pleasure of your company
in the
MARITIME GALLERY
Where relics of the ship
UNICORN
Are on display

Marlinspike Hall.

Well, what do you say, now, my friends? All's well that ends well, eh?

Just as I always said: more to the west!

Yes, yes. But I said: all's well that ends well. Don't you agree?

Your maritime gallery? . . . I think it is very successful!

Thanks. But I was just saying that our adventures had a happy ending. They've ended, and happily! . . .

No thank you. Never between meals.

No, no! Blistering barnacles! All's well that ends well! ALL'S WELL THAT ENDS WELL!

Without any doubt!

. . . and this is just the moment to quote that old saying: All's well that ends well!

HERGÉ.

HERGÉ
★
THE ADVENTURES OF
TINTIN
★

THE SEVEN
CRYSTAL BALLS

LITTLE, BROWN AND COMPANY
New York Boston

THE SEVEN CRYSTAL BALLS

HOME AFTER TWO YEARS

Sanders-Hardiman Expedition Returns

LIVERPOOL, *Thursday*. The seven members of the Sanders-Hardiman Ethnographic Expedition landed at Liverpool today. Back in Europe after a fruitful two-year trip through Peru and Bolivia, the scientists report that their travels took them deep into little-known territory. They discovered several Inca tombs, one of which contained a mummy still wearing a 'borla' or royal crown of solid gold. Funerary inscriptions establish beyond doubt that the tomb belonged to the Inca Rascar Capac.

This will lead to trouble . . . You see if it doesn't!

What'll lead to trouble?

All this mummy business. Remember, young man, what happened with Tut-Ankh-Amen!

Think of all those Egyptologists, dying in mysterious circumstances after they'd opened the tomb of the Pharaoh . . . You wait, the same will happen to those busy-bodies, violating the Inca's burial chamber.

You think so?

I'm sure of it! . . . Anyway, why can't they leave them in peace? . . . What'd we say if the Egyptians or the Peruvians came over here and started digging up our kings? . . . What'd we say then, eh?

Well, I . . .

Oh . . . excuse me. I see we're coming to my station . . . I must go.

Here we are . . .

Good morning, Nestor. Is the Captain at home?

No, Mr Tintin, the master is out at the moment. He went riding . . .

But he won't be long now. Look . . . You see . . .

Here comes his horse . . .

!

And there's the master.

Hello, Captain! . . .

Good day, my dear sir, good day. Excuse me for just a   moment . . .

Nestor! . . . Nestor! . . . Bring me another, please!

Coming, sir . . .

Thank you, Nestor.

'Pon my word, it's Tintin! . . . Delighted to see you, my dear chap!

What fair wind brings you here?

I just dropped in to say hello . . . to you and Professor Calculus . . . How is he?

Oh, he's fine . . . Here he comes now . . . Still crazy about his dowsing, as you see . . . The dear fellow is convinced that there's a Saxon burial-ground in the neighbourhood, so he's decided to find it.

Hello, Professor Calculus.

Why, it's our good friend Tintin! What a delightful surprise!

You're staying with us for some time, I hope?

I'm afraid not. I have to go home this evening.

Excellent! Excellent! What good news! Nothing could please me more.

Well, I'll see you later . . . I must get on with my work . . .

Let's leave the old boy to his treasure-hunt, while we have a drink.

Apropos of a drink . . . I've just remembered . . .

!

Come with me. I've got something amazing to show you . . .

After you, I insist . . .

Bravo, Nestor! Bravo!

WOOAH! WOOAH!

Wooah! . . . Wooah!

FFFFFH WOOAH GRR SCHH

You see, you miserable animal! That's your handiwork!

Oh, don't bother about him. Come with me . . .

You're going to see something fantastic!

Here we are.

Now, my dear fellow, just keep your eyes open.

First, another monocle . . .

There . . . Now, watch . . . I begin by pouring plain water into this glass . . . Note that; nothing but plain water.

Now, pay attention . . . This is it. Watch me very closely. I'm going to begin.

You see this? I have here a hollow cardboard cylinder . . . Hollow, you understand. Look . . . There's nothing inside, is there?

No, it seems quite empty.

Good . . . I place the cylinder over the glass . . . The glass which contains . . . Contains what?

Plain water.

Water, exactly . . . And now, quiet please! Watch carefully!

!

Presto!

And, voilà! . . . Now, would you kindly tell me, what have we in the glass under there?

In the glass? Water, I suppose.

Water! . . . HAHAHAHAHA! . . . Don't make me laugh! . . . HAHAHA! . . . This'll kill me! . . . HAHA! . . . Have a look! . . . Lift up the cylinder.

HAHAHAHA! . . . Water! . . . HOHOHOHO! . . . HAHAHAHA!

HAHAHAHA!   HOHOHOHO!

?   HAHAHAHAHA!

I'm sorry, Captain, but there's something here I don't quite get. You see, it still is water in this glass . . .

Water! . . . That's a good one! . . . Water! . . . You're a real comic! . . . Water, he says! . . .

Billions of bilious blue blistering barnacles in a thundering typhoon! It IS water!

72

But what on earth did you expect it to be?

Whisky, by thunder! . . . Whisky!

Whisky? . . . Come now, Captain, you can't be serious. How in the world could water turn itself into whisky? . . . It's impossible!

Impossible! Impossible! . . . No, blistering barnacles, it's not impossible. He manages it every time!

Who's he?

Bruno, the master magician! He's appearing at the Hippodrome. I've studied his act for a solid fortnight, trying to discover how he does it . . .

Yesterday I thought I'd solved it at last. Blistering barnacles, what do I get? Water, water, and still more water! But I'm going back again tonight, and you're coming too! This time I'll get the answer!

HIPPOD

You must watch carefully to see exactly what he does . . .

We've got plenty of time. There are several other turns before he comes on.

First we have Ragdalam the fakir, with Yamilah, the amazing clairvoyant. Then Ramon Zarate, the knife-thrower. Next . . .

Ssh! Here comes Ragdalam the fakir. He's incredible too.

Ladies and gentlemen, I have much pleasure in inviting you to participate in a remarkable experiment: an experiment I had the honour to conduct . . .

. . . before his Highness the Maharaja of Hambalapur, and for which he invested me with the Order of the Grand Naja . . . The secret of the mysterious power at my command was entrusted to me by the famous yogi, Chandra Patnagar Rabad . . . And now, ladies and gentlemen, it is my privilege to introduce to you one of the most amazing personalities of the twentieth century . . .

I present: Madame Yamilah!

First I will put Madame Yamilah into a hypnotic trance . . .

Madame Yamilah, are you ready to answer me?

Yes, master . . .

Good . . . Tell me, Madame Yamilah, what is this gentleman's Christian name?

Augustus.

Is that correct, sir?

Yes . . . quite correct!

Good . . . Now tell me, Madame Yamilah, what is in this lady's handbag?

A handkerchief, some keys . . . a diary . . . a powder compact . . . a driving licence . . .

And the number on that licence, Madame Yamilah?

Seven six eight one three seven . . .

Absolutely right!

Fantastic, isn't it?

Madame Yamilah, will you please tell me whether that lady there in the third row is married.

Yes, she is married.

Good . . . And what is her husband's profession?

Photographer.

Is that right, madam?

Quite right.

I see him . . . returning from a long journey to a distant land . . . He . . . he . . . What is happening? . . . He is ill . . . very ill . . . with a mysterious sickness . . .

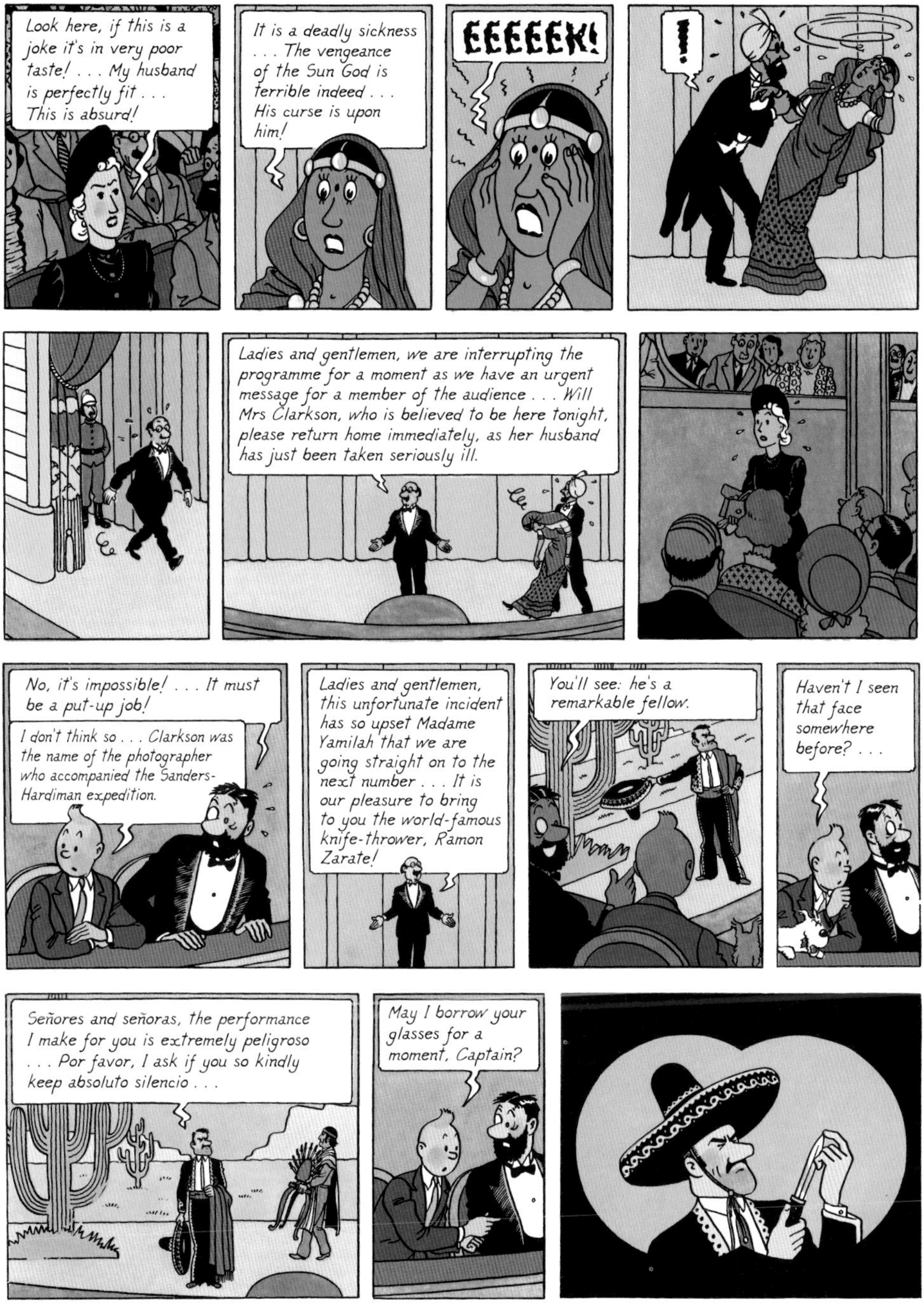

Look here, if this is a joke it's in very poor taste! . . . My husband is perfectly fit . . . This is absurd!
It is a deadly sickness . . . The vengeance of the Sun God is terrible indeed . . . His curse is upon him!
EEEEEK!
!
Ladies and gentlemen, we are interrupting the programme for a moment as we have an urgent message for a member of the audience . . . Will Mrs Clarkson, who is believed to be here tonight, please return home immediately, as her husband has just been taken seriously ill.
No, it's impossible! . . . It must be a put-up job!
I don't think so . . . Clarkson was the name of the photographer who accompanied the Sanders-Hardiman expedition.
Ladies and gentlemen, this unfortunate incident has so upset Madame Yamilah that we are going straight on to the next number . . . It is our pleasure to bring to you the world-famous knife-thrower, Ramon Zarate!
You'll see: he's a remarkable fellow.
Haven't I seen that face somewhere before? . . .
Señores and señoras, the performance I make for you is extremely peligroso . . . Por favor, I ask if you so kindly keep absoluto silencio . . .
May I borrow your glasses for a moment, Captain?

Great snakes! It's General Alcazar! . . .

General who?

Alcazar . . . You remember, he used to be President of the Republic of San Theodoros. I wonder what's landed him on the music-hall stage.

Now, is muy dificil!

Is more dificil!

Now, is mucho more dificil!

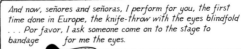

And now, señores and señoras, I perform for you, the first time done in Europe, the knife-throw with the eyes blindfold . . . Por favor, I ask someone come on to the stage to bandage for me the eyes.

There, that's it.

Muchas gracias, señor . . .

It almost went wrong three nights ago! The knife landed just on the edge of the target. Half an inch further and that Indian would have been skewered!

¿Esta usted?

¡si!

¡Muy bien!

Well, what do you think? Amazing, wasn't it?

Yes, it was very good.

Let's see what's coming next... Here we are... Good heavens!

Look, Bianca Castafiore, the Milanese nightingale!

Yes, I thought you'd be surprised!

She turns up in the oddest places: Syldavia, Borduria, the Red Sea... She seems to follow us around!

I know; she's indefatigable! Here she comes!...

Ladies and gentlemen, tonight by special request I would like to sing for you the Jewel Song from "Faust".

Ah, my beauty past compare, These jewels bright I wear

Powerful stuff, eh?

You've said it!

I don't know why, but whenever I hear her it reminds me of a hurricane that hit my ship – when I was sailing in the West Indies some years ago...

Come reply! Mirror, mirror, tell me truly! Reply! Reply!

WOW-OW-WOOOW-OOOW

! !

WOOW-WOOOOW-OW-OW-OW-OOOW!

?

NO! NO! IT IS NOT

77

She's in very good voice tonight.

Snowy wasn't bad either.

Look here, why don't we go and say hello to General Alcazar in his dressing room?

That's a good idea!

This way?

I think so.

NO ENTRY

Are you sure this is right?

We'll soon find out . . .

Where are we?

I don't know . . .

KEEP OUT

Ah, there's someone; they'll probably be able to direct us.

Excuse me, sir, can you tell me where I can find General . . . I mean Ramon Zarate?

Down the passage, Dressing Room 14.

You saw who it was?

Yes . . . the fakir and Madame Yamilah.

Number 14 . . . Down the passage . . .

Look, here we are.

RACING SPECIAL

RAT TAT TAT TAT

14

Come in!

14

Hello, General Alcazar!

14

RAMO

Don't you remember me?

Caramba! . . . Tintin! . . . My old friend! . . . Amigo mio, qué sorpresa! . . . Ay! Dios de mi vida! How I am happy to see you again.

And this person here is what?

You remember, my friend Captain Haddock.

Los amigos de nuestros amigos son nuestros amigos! . . . I am happy Señor Colonel, so happy!

Delighted!

Descuida, no es la policia . . .

Ah! Bueno!

Poor Chiquito! . . . You understand . . . Ever since police come to look at our passports and our papers, he find police everywhere.

Yes, I quite see.

Por favor, we celebrate this happy meeting. You take with me a glass of aguardiente.

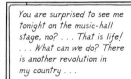

Your good health, amigo mio! Your good health, Señor Colonel!

Here's to you, General!

Good health!

Look out, it's awfully strong!

Strong? . . . Pooh! . . . I'm used to it, my dear fellow . . .

You are surprised to see me tonight on the music-hall stage, no? . . . That is life! . . . What can we do? There is another revolution in my country . . .

. . . and that mangy dog, General Tapioca, has seized power. So, I must leave San Theodoros. After I try many different jobs, I become a knife-thrower.

Sorry to interrupt, but it's time we were getting back to our seats; otherwise we'll miss the conjuror.

Yes, you're right.

I'm very sorry we have to leave you so soon. You see, we rather want to watch the conjuror do his act . . . Goodbye, General.

Adios, amigo mio.

Quick, or we shall miss the turn!

I don't remember coming this way.

Yes, yes...

Look . . . there's the door to the bar.

BAR

Thundering typhoons! . . . A piece of scenery!

BAR

Let's see, was it this way?

BANG BOOM

!

Billions of blue blistering boiled and barbecued barnacles!

Thousands of thundering typhoons! All because of that second-rate son of a sword-swallower!

Still, I mustn't let it get me down.

Help! Help!

Captain!

Stop, Captain, stop!

BOOM

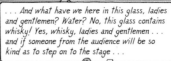

. . . And what have we here in this glass, ladies and gentlemen? Water? No, this glass contains whisky! Yes, whisky, ladies and gentlemen . . . and if someone from the audience will be so kind as to step on to the stage . . .

BOOM
DONG
DING-DONG
BING

?

DONG   DONG
DONG

BOOM

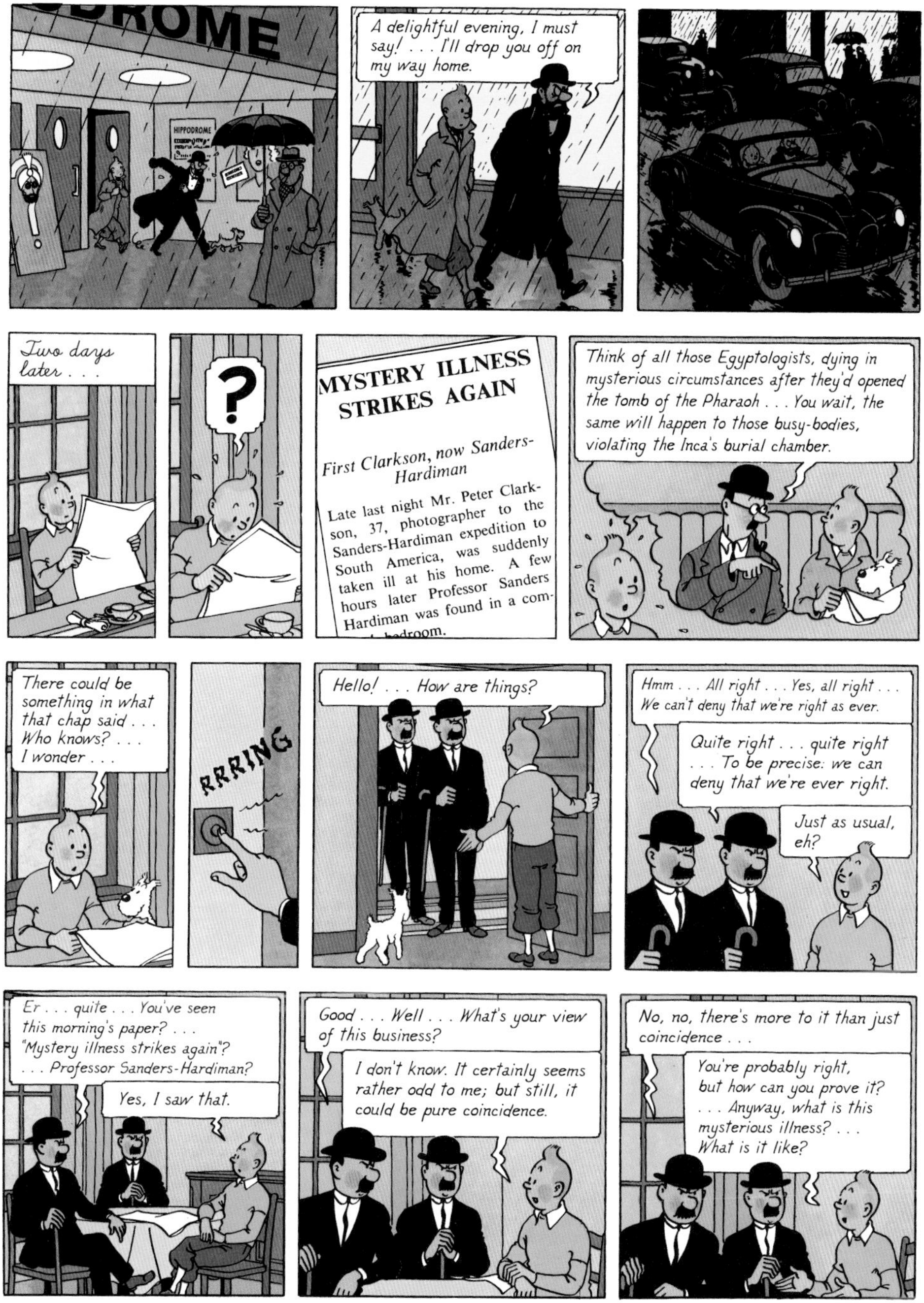

HIPPODROME
A delightful evening, I must say! . . . I'll drop you off on my way home.
Two days later . . .
?
MYSTERY ILLNESS STRIKES AGAIN
First Clarkson, now Sanders-Hardiman
Late last night Mr. Peter Clarkson, 37, photographer to the Sanders-Hardiman expedition to South America, was suddenly taken ill at his home. A few hours later Professor Sanders Hardiman was found in a com-
bedroom.
Think of all those Egyptologists, dying in mysterious circumstances after they'd opened the tomb of the Pharaoh . . . You wait, the same will happen to those busy-bodies, violating the Inca's burial chamber.
There could be something in what that chap said . . . Who knows? . . . I wonder . . .
RRRING
Hello! . . . How are things?
Hmm . . . All right . . . Yes, all right . . . We can't deny that we're right as ever.
Quite right . . . quite right . . . To be precise: we can deny that we're ever right.
Just as usual, eh?
Er . . . quite . . . You've seen this morning's paper? . . . "Mystery illness strikes again"? . . . Professor Sanders-Hardiman?
Yes, I saw that.
Good . . . Well . . . What's your view of this business?
I don't know. It certainly seems rather odd to me; but still, it could be pure coincidence.
No, no, there's more to it than just coincidence . . .
You're probably right, but how can you prove it? . . . Anyway, what is this mysterious illness? . . . What is it like?

Strictly speaking, it isn't exactly an illness . . . The two victims were found asleep: one at his desk, the other in his library. According to a preliminary report, the explorers seem to have fallen into some sort of deep coma or hypnotic sleep . . .

Oh? How very strange . . .

But have a look here . . .

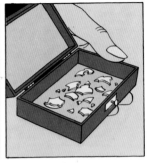

Well? . . . They're little pieces of glass.

Pieces of crystal . . . they were found close to the two victims.

Have you thought of having these crystal fragments analysed?

Yes, I've left some of them at the laboratory at police headquarters. They're working on them now.

There it is: that's all we know so far.

Anyway, it's enough for us to rule out the theory of simple coincidence . . . What we need now is the result of the police analysis. I wonder . . .

I'll ring up the laboratory. Perhaps they've got the answer already.

Good.

Hello? . . . Headquarters? . . . Put me through to the laboratory, please . . . Hello, Doctor Simons? . . . This is Thomson . . . No, without a P, as in Venezuela . . . Yes . . . the analysis . . . Well?

What??

Professor Reedbuck! . . . It's fantastic! . . . Found asleep in his bath . . . Yes . . . They discovered the same crystal fragments . . . Incredible! . . . I say, how is the analysis getting on? . . . Have you . . . ?

Nothing definite yet . . . We've established that the glass particles come from little crystal balls . . . These probably contained the substance . . .

. . . which sent the unfortunate victims into a sort of coma . . . The substance? We have absolutely no idea . . . Yes, we're pressing on with our tests . . . I'll let you know how things are going. Goodbye.

I can't believe it! Professor Bathtub, found asleep in the reeds!

Number three!

We must warn the other members of the expedition at once! And we must get police protection for them.

Why? . . . You don't think that they . . . that we . . . that it . . . ?

Of course! There's no reason why this should stop. Everyone who took part in the expedition is in danger. Let's see . . . Sanders-Hardiman, Clarkson, Reedbuck: that's three . . . Who were the others? . . . Oh yes! Mark Falconer. Ring up Mark Falconer.

Hello? . . . Hello? . . . Hello? . . . Hello?

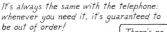

It's always the same with the telephone: whenever you need it, it's guaranteed to be out of order!

There's no reply?

I hate to interfere, but if I were you I'd try using that.

Is that Mark Falconer?

Yes, Falconer speaking . . .

Yes . . . yes . . . yes, I was just reading the paper . . . What? Professor Reedbuck too? . . . And . . . no . . . What's that? Crystal fragments! . . . By Jupiter, so he was telling the truth!

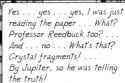

Who? . . . An old Indian, who got drunk on coca one night. He told me . . . No, I can't explain over the telephone . . . No, I'll come along and see you . . . Where? . . . Good!

I'll pick up a taxi and be with you right away. Meanwhile, warn Cantonneau, Midge and Tarragon. Tell them to stay indoors. And above all to keep away from the windows . . . Yes, windows . . . Me? Don't worry, I shall be on my guard . . . Goodbye for now. I'll be with you soon.

He's coming here. He seemed to know all about it . . . He said we should warn the other explorers, telling them not to go out, and to keep away from the windows.

Good, I'll warn Professor Cantonneau . . .

Great snakes! I can't get through! I must keep on trying!

If they put in an appearance, I'll be ready!

Taxi!

Twenty-six, Labrador Road . . .

Right you are, sir.

Hello? . . . Ah, it's you, Professor Cantonneau. Thank goodness I've caught you in time!

My dear Tintin, what's the matter? . . . No, I've not heard anything . . . I . . . What? But that's fantastic! . . . And Clarkson too? . . . And Reedbuck? . . . How terrible! . . . What? I must be on my guard?

Yes, be very careful . . . And above all, don't go near the window . . . Yes, the window . . . It's . . .

ZZINGG
OH! . . . CLING
CLING CLING
CLING

Hello? . . . Hello Professor Cantonneau! . . . Hello? . . . Hello? . . . Hello?

What's happened?

Hello? . . . Hello? . . .

Something's happened to Professor Cantonneau! . . . I'm going straight round there . . . You stay here and warn the other two explorers at once.

There's a taxi pulling up outside the door.

I expect it's brought Mr Falconer . . . I'll take it on.

Hurry, Snowy! Hurry!

Here we are, sir: sixty-five pence . . .

?

!

The same crystal fragments!

Your passenger – he's been attacked! Tell me, did you stop anywhere on the way?

No . . . oh, yes. Once, at a junction, when the lights were against me.

Now I remember! It must have happened then . . . Another taxi drew up alongside mine, and I heard a faint sound of glass breaking. I didn't think much of it at the time. The lights changed, and we moved off.

I see. Go into the house and up to the first floor, where you'll find two police officers. Tell them your story. I'm off to warn Doctor Midge.

Righto!

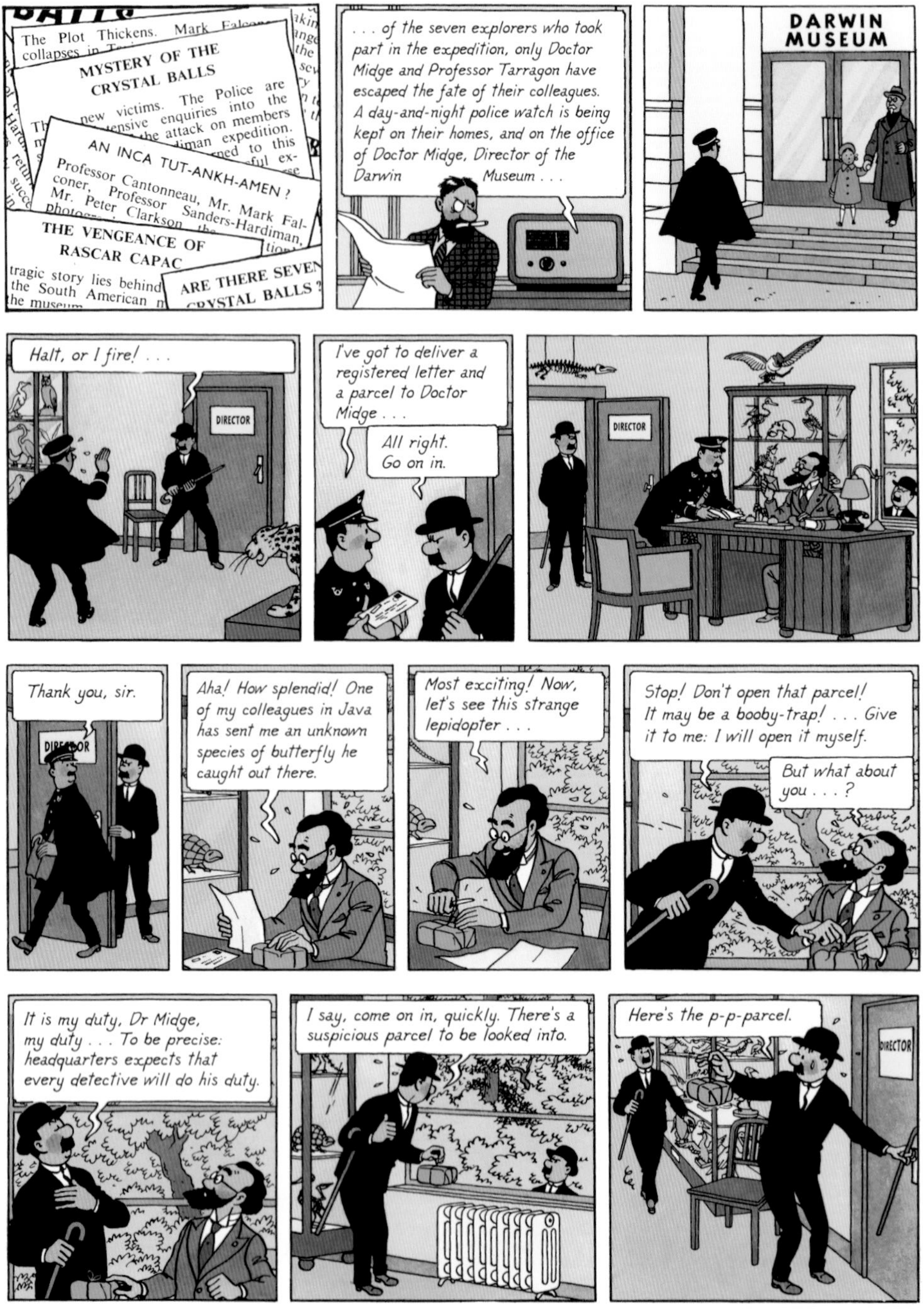
MYSTERY OF THE CRYSTAL BALLS
AN INCA TUT-ANKH-AMEN ?
THE VENGEANCE OF RASCAR CAPAC
ARE THERE SEVEN CRYSTAL BALLS ?
. . . of the seven explorers who took part in the expedition, only Doctor Midge and Professor Tarragon have escaped the fate of their colleagues. A day-and-night police watch is being kept on their homes, and on the office of Doctor Midge, Director of the Darwin Museum . . .
DARWIN MUSEUM
Halt, or I fire! . . .
DIRECTOR
I've got to deliver a registered letter and a parcel to Doctor Midge . . .
All right. Go on in.
DIRECTOR
Thank you, sir.
Aha! How splendid! One of my colleagues in Java has sent me an unknown species of butterfly he caught out there.
Most exciting! Now, let's see this strange lepidopter . . .
Stop! Don't open that parcel! It may be a booby-trap! . . . Give it to me: I will open it myself.
But what about you . . . ?
It is my duty, Dr Midge, my duty . . . To be precise: headquarters expects that every detective will do his duty.
I say, come on in, quickly. There's a suspicious parcel to be looked into.
Here's the p-p-parcel.
DIRECTOR

We'd b-b-better open it . . . Keep c-c-calm!

That's right: keep c-c-calm!

C-c-careful! . . .

C-c-careful! . . .

DIRECTOR

Whew! It's all right: false alarm . . . It's just a butterfly . . . And what a butterfly! . . . Look . . .

It's magnificent!

SPECIMEN CAPTURED IN JAVA

Between ourselves, let's face it – that was a narrow escape . . .

Between ourselves, to be precise: I agree!

DIREC

Ssh! Someone's coming

DIREC

Hello, all well?

Ah, it's Tintin.

DIRECTOR

Yes, all's well. But we had a narrow escape. We've just opened a parcel which looked rather suspicious. Luckily, it was only a butterfly. Look, here it is . . .

What a beauty!

ECTOR

Good. I see Dr Midge's door is well guarded. What about his window?

His window? I'm guarding that. What more need I say?

TOR

You're guarding his window? Then what are you doing in here?

Great Scotland Yard, I . . .

CTOR

ZZING CLING CLING

DIRECTOR

89

Goodness gracious! He's asleep too!

ZZZZ ZZZZ

Over there! Someone's just disappeared into the shrubbery!

Hello, Headquarters? . . . This is Thompson . . . Yes, with a P, as in Philadelphia . . . . Yes . . . I'm very well, thank you . . . It's Dr Midge who isn't . . . I mean . . . Yes, sir . . . They've got him too.

That way, Snowy! . . . Hurry! . . . Hurry!

After him, Snowy! . . . Catch him!

CRACK

Wooah! Wooah!

All right, Snowy! . . . Hang on! . . . I'm coming!

WOOAH

CRACK

Here I come! . . . Don't let him go! . . .

Wooah! Wooah!

A cat! All that fuss for a miserable cat! Meanwhile, of course, our quarry has got clean away . . . Come on now, get going!

The next morning . . .

Extraordinary! . . . Quite extraordinary! . . . Another victim . . . It's amazing!

No, I think it's a little to the left.

No, I said: another victim. Here in the newspaper . . . The Director of the Darwin Museum . . . Doctor Midge.

Not yet, but I'm sure to get there in the end.

Daily Reporter

MYSTERY OF THE CRYSTAL BALLS

Director of Darwin Museum is new victim

DR. MIDGE IN COMA

Yes. Good. There. Read it yourself . . . It's simpler that way . . .

Extraordinary! . . . Quite extraordinary . . . Have you read this? . . . No? . . . I'm surprised . . . The headlines are printed quite large . . . Never mind: I'll read it to you myself . . .

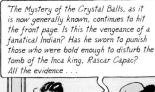

"The Mystery of the Crystal Balls, as it is now generally known, continues to hit the front page. Is this the vengeance of a fanatical Indian? Has he sworn to punish those who were bold enough to disturb the tomb of the Inca king, Rascar Capac? All the evidence . . .

. . . points that way, and this dramatic theory cannot be discounted. But it poses new questions. Why did the mysterious avenger not kill his victims on the spot? Why, instead, plunge them into a profound sleep? . . .

RRRING

. . . a sleep which, says medical opinion, could be prolonged for an indefinite period without imperilling their lives. Readers are already familiar with the details of the . . ."

Good morning, Nestor. Is the Captain at home?

Yes, sir . . . Come in.

!

Wooah! Wooah!

Pffft!

Tintin, my dear fellow!
... How very nice!

How are you? And how's
Professor Calculus?

Very well. He's busy
reading the paper
to me ...

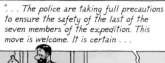

"... The police are taking full precautions
to ensure the safety of the last of the
seven members of the expedition. This
move is welcome. It is certain ...

... that otherwise he would
swiftly share the fate of his
colleagues. Today, Professor
Tarragon ..." Oh!

Tarragon! ... The last of the
seven? ... Is it really him? Well I
never, I know Tarragon ... He and
I were students together ...

You know Professor Tarragon, the expert on
ancient America? ... Isn't he the one with
the Rascar Capac mummy in his possession?

Oh, no! On the contrary, he's
most kind ... I'll introduce you
to him if you like.

I'd enjoy meeting him.
Thank you.

You'd like to go now?
... Certainly ...
Come along ...

Look, visitors for Professor
Tarragon.

We'd like to see Professor
Tarragon ...

Have you
a pass?

Haddock, Tintin and
Calculus .... Right.
Wait here, and I'll
see if you can go in.

It's like trying to get into
a fortress!

We have our orders
...

OK, these gentlemen
can come in.

They're certainly looking after the professor!

Blistering barnacles, it's hot!

Yes. I think there's a storm brewing . . .

RAT TAT TAT

Come in!

Here we are, Professor. Here are your visitors.

Hello, Hercules!

Cuthbert!

Well, well; dear old Cuthbert!

My dear Hercules, I've brought two of my friends to meet you . . .

Welcome, gentlemen, welcome!

Let me introduce Captain Haddock, retired from the sea . . .

How d'you do.

And this is my young friend Tintin, the famous reporter . . .

A grip like a mangle!

Delighted.

Wooah! Wooah!

What's the matter, Snowy? What's up?

?

93

HA - HA - HA - HA - HA!

Here's the culprit . . . Our friend Rascar Capac frightened your dog . . . Rascar Capac: he-who-unleashes-the-fire-of-heaven.

BOOM

What about that! We were just talking about Rascar Capac, he-who-unleashes-the-fire-of-heaven, and I think he's going to oblige: look . . .

You have an open car, I believe . . . If I were you, I'd put it under cover right away. These summer storms can be very violent . . . an absolute downpour . . .

Thanks. May I put it in the garage?

Did you hear that? . . . Sounded like a shot outside . . .

BANG

Over there . . . a man running . . . It's one of the detectives guarding the house . . .

Quick, let's see what's happening . . .

That came from the direction of the gates.

BANG

What were those two shots?

There weren't any shots. You made the mistake of leaving your car in the blazing sun . . . Look, your tyres have burst!

Well, what was it?

Nothing: just a couple of tyres bursting.

A couple of tyres . . . a couple of tyres on my car! . . . Blistering barnacles, and you call that nothing?

BANG

Blue blistering barnacles in a thundering typhoon!

Now what are we going to do? Two tyres: and I've only got one spare!

It's quite simple: you spend the night here . . . then tomorrow morning you can phone the garage.

This is it: here comes the rain. Let's get indoors, quickly!

BOM BROM BOBOM

Excuse me, Hercules, but I think there's someone knocking at the door.

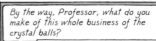
Everything all right? . . . Good, good . . . At any rate, the false alarm did prove that the house is well guarded.

Yes, it certainly seems to be. But still, we must be very careful.

By the way, Professor, what do you make of this whole business of the crystal balls?

What do I make of it? . . . Not much . . . But, as a matter of fact, I've drafted a paper . . .

. . . on the occult practices of ancient Peru. It seems to have some bearing, but I doubt if it will solve our problem.

Look at this . . . it's a translation of part of the inscriptions carved on the walls of Rascar Capac's tomb . . . You may like to read it.

"After many moons will come seven strangers with pale faces; they will profane the sacred dwellings of he-who-unleashes-the-fire-of-heaven. These vandals will carry the body of the Inca to their own far country. But the curse of the gods will be as their shadow and pursue them over land and sea . . ."

But . . . but . . . this is quite extraordinary!

Isn't it? . . . But read the next bit . . .

CRACK

BANG

Good lord! . . . The mummy!

Rascar Capac's disappeared! . . .
Vaporized! . . . Vanished into thin air!
There's nothing left but the jewels!

But Professor Tarragon . . .
what's the matter?

I . . . it's nothing . . .
Read the rest . . . the
rest of my translation.

"There will come a day when Rascar Capac
will bring down upon himself the cleansing
fire. In one moment of flame he will return
to his true element; on that day will
punishment descend upon the desecrators."

Excuse me, Hercules.

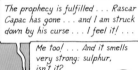

The prophecy is fulfilled . . . Rascar
Capac has gone . . . and I am struck
down by his curse . . . I feel it! . . .

Me too! . . . And it smells
very strong: sulphur,
isn't it?

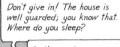

Don't give in! The house is
well guarded; you know that.
Where do you sleep?

In the next room.
There are no windows.

Good. And there are shutters in here . . .
What's more, we are upstairs. To make
doubly sure, we'll station two policemen
outside these windows . . . You see,
there's absolutely no danger.

You're right . . . I'm being
absurd . . . Let me show you
to your rooms, then I'll bid
you good-night.

Some hours later . . .

Whew! What a relief . . . It was only a dream . . . The gale blew the window open!

Still, it was a horrible nightmare!

HELP! . . . HELP!

That's the Captain's voice!

THUMP

What's happened, Captain? . . . I thought I heard you shouting.

Yes, I . . . I had a frightful nightmare! . . . Rascar Capac came into my room . . . He had a huge crystal ball in his hand . . . he hurled it down on the floor . . .

Incredible! . . . The same dream as mine!

OOH OOH

Now what is it?

Look out! . . . He's there! . . . He's after me! . . . He's coming! . . .

99

He's there, I tell you! ... It's him ... the Indian from downstairs! ... He came into my room ... he was brandishing a huge crystal ball!

Good heavens! It's the same dream again! ... How fantastic!

All the same, let's have a look ...

You see? ... No one! ... He was only dreaming, like us.

Snowy! ... Look at Snowy!

Strange! ... He's certainly smelt something.

Look, he's going down the stairs. I wonder what ...

Ssh! ... Quiet!

Mind the carpet!

?

BANG BING BONKABONK

Billions of blue bilious blistering barnacles in a thundering typhoon!

Good heavens, Captain, are you all right?

You're lucky, I must say . . .

You could have broken your neck!

Thundering typhoons! Sssh!

Wowowow! Wowooowow!

What is it?

I don't know . . . Snowy began howling outside Professor Tarragon's door . . .

Professor Tarragon! Professor Tarragon!

He doesn't answer . . . Break down the door!

THUD
THUD

CRASH

Great snakes! I only hope . . .

False alarm! He's still fast asleep . . .

?

CRUNCH

Too late! . . . Look there: fragments of crystal!

But it's impossible . . . every single exit is guarded . . .

Professor Tarragon! Professor Tarragon!

There's nothing we can do . . . The crystal ball has done its work . . . and claimed the last of the seven.

ZZZZ. . . ZZZZ . . .

Quick, the window! . . . The intruder must have gone that way!

But no . . . the window and the shutter are closed tight . . . it's incredible!

Has anyone gone past you?

No, sir, no one at all . . . Why?

This absolutely beats me . . . How did the fellow make his getaway?

Oh! Look over there! Rascar Capac's jewels have disappeared!

WOOAH! WOOAH!

There! That's how it was done . . . the attacker came and went by the chimney!

Wooah! Wooah!

Well, if he went up here, there's still time – he can't have got clean away . . .

Well, now we know! He did use the chimney!

The roof! . . . Search the roof!

Very good, sir!

Over there! . . . Look! . . . There's a man running away!

Got him!

He's fallen! Quick, let's see . . .

He fell somewhere about here . . .

Seek, Snowy! Seek him out!

There's nothing I'd like better, but . . .

Oh, so that's it! Snowy's nose is still caked with soot . . . He can't possibly smell anything else!

AAAAAAAAAAAH!

That was Professor Tarragon's voice!

Blistering barnacles! They're murdering him! . . . Come on, hurry!

Help!

AAAH!

Mercy! . . . Mercy!

They're coming back! . . . I can see them! They're going to smother me!

Keep away, you devils! They'll tear me to pieces!

It's all right, Professor Tarragon, it's all right . . . There's no one here . . . only your friends.

But now what? . . . Look, he's fallen back into a coma.

No luck, the thug escaped us . . . Now, I wonder what's going on back here at the house.

He screamed and shouted: he seemed to be suffering horribly . . . Then suddenly he calmed down . . . I think it would be an idea to call in a doctor.

The next morning . . .

Hmm . . . yes . . . It's certainly a clear case of acute coma . . . Look, his muscles are absolutely relaxed, his limbs completely inert . . .

?

YEOW!

They're coming back! . . . They'll start again – tormenting me! . . . Help, help!

They're coming! . . . Get away, you torturers! . . . Help me! . . . Help!

Who is it?

RAT TAT TAT

Oh, it's you? . . . Good morning . . . Is Hercules there?

Yes, he's there, in bed, ill. The doctor is here . . . He sounds in a bad state.

Going round the estate? . . . Good, I'll join him.

Where is he?

I can't see him.

Still, that's easy. I'll find him with   my pendulum.

Hello, what's happening?

Peculiar, very peculiar! I wonder . . .

Hat, umbrella, spectacles, pendulum; that's the lot: on we go! . . .

Goodness gracious! How extraordinary! There must be something behind these bushes.

?

Well, well, well . . .
What have we here?

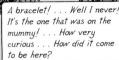

A bracelet! . . . Well I never!
It's the one that was on the
mummy! . . . How very
curious . . . How did it come
to be here?

Magnificent! . . . It's
obviously made of solid
gold . . . I'll put it on and
go indoors wearing it,
and see if they notice . . .

Really splendid . . .
And how well it goes
with   my coat!

A few minutes later . . .

Calculus? . . . Out in the garden
. . . I expect he's hard at work
with his pendulum. Wait; I'll go
and find him.

Now where's old
Cuthbert got to?

Strange, I'm sure he
said he was going
into the   garden.

Hello . . . Did you find him?

No, he wasn't there.
He's probably back in
his room . . . I'll go up
and look . . .

No, he's not in his room.
That's rather odd . . .

Let's go back into the garden. I expect
we'll find him in the shrubbery with
that beloved pendulum of his.

CALCULUS!
CALCULUS!

It's no good
shouting for _him!_

Now where's the old goat hidden
himself? . . . Calculus!!!

CALCULUS!

?

Captain! . . . Captain! Look up there!

Bloodstains! The imprint of a hand! . . . What does that mean? Who could have . . .

Who? . . . The intruder last night, I'll bet . . . No wonder we couldn't find him . . . Wounded, and chased like that, he didn't know which way to turn . . . so he took refuge in the top of this tree . . .

But . . . he could still be up there . . .

You're right . . . I'm going to see for myself . . .

Do be careful . . . Take my gun with you.

Good idea. Thanks . . .

Any luck?

No, I still can't see anything . . .

CRACK

I'm all right, Captain . . . only a rotten branch breaking . . .

You're all right, eh? What about me?

There's no one here now. I'm coming down.

Captain! . . . Over there, to your right, look! . . . More to the right . . . more . . . There, you've got it!

It's Calculus's umbrella!

It is his, isn't it?

Yes, of course it is! How in the . . .

Look there . . . The grass is all trampled down.

And these broken branches . . . There's been a fight here!

A fight? . . . Old Calculus been fighting?

Maybe not . . . But he's certainly been attacked . . . Now I see what happened . . . The intruder was still up in the tree . . . Along came Calculus . . . and the other fellow jumped on him.

But, blistering barnacles, why? Why on earth should anyone attack Calculus?

I don't know, Captain, I don't know. All I do know is that Professor Calculus has disappeared, and we've got to find him.

SNOWY! SNOWY! SNOWY!

Snowy! Snowy! Snowy!

You can have your bone back in a minute, Snowy. But first of all you must try to find the Professor.

Seek, Snowy, seek him out! . . . Go on . . . Quickly!

Is he in there?

Look out, Captain! . . . Look out! Take cover!

Why? . . . What is it?

Take cover!

BANG BANG

Cannibals! . . . Caterpillars! . . . Troglodytes! . . . Tramps! . . . Ectoplasms! . . . Sea-gherkins!

Captain! . . . I'm going to crawl round to the summer-house. You fire a shot from time to time . . . Here's your gun . . . I'll throw it across . . .

There!

Thanks!

Now, my fine fellow, see how you like this!

BANG

CRACK

BANG

BANG

If I could just get that bone back . . . Steady now! Wait for it . . .

BANG

Ha! ha! So I got it! . . . Smart work, eh?

BANG

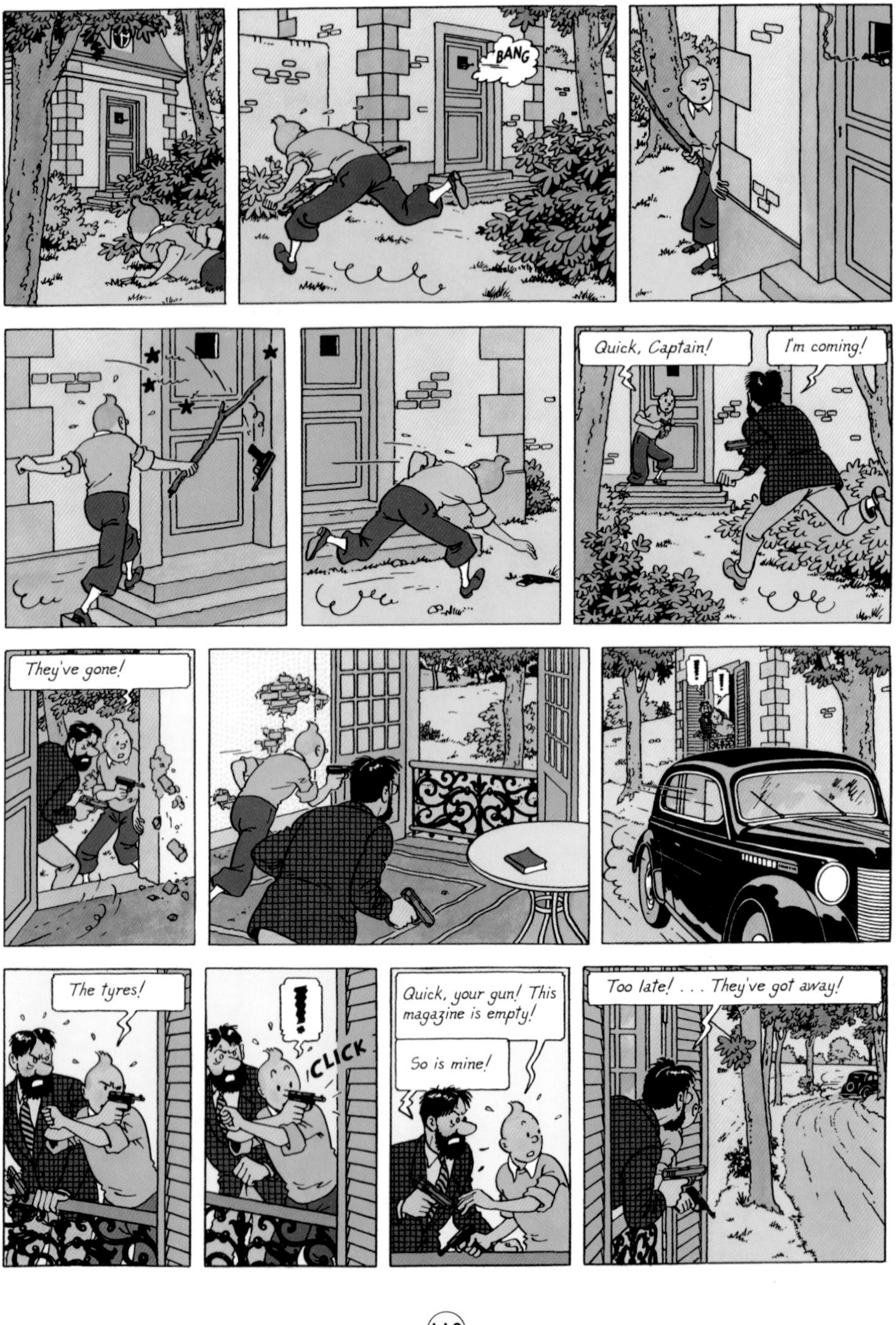

BANG
Quick, Captain!
I'm coming!
They've gone!
The tyres!
CLICK
Quick, your gun! This magazine is empty!
So is mine!
Too late! . . . They've got away!

Tribe of savages! . . . Vampires! . . . Monsters!

Here, Captain . . . I've got the car number . . . We're not beaten yet . . . Come on, quickly! . . .

The inspector will pass the number on to his headquarters at once . . .

The rats!

Hello, Headquarters? This is Chambers . . . Yes . . . One of Professor Tarragon's friends has been kidnapped . . . Professor Cuthbert Calculus . . . Yes, in a car . . . I'll give you its number and a description . . .

An Opel.

Headquarters to all stations. Calling all cars. Arrest occupants of black saloon car, model Opel Olympia, registration number 317413, proceeding from Harlesford in a south-westerly direction.

The brutes! . . . Kidnapping Calculus! . . . And why, may I ask? . . . What possible reason can they have for kidnapping poor Cuthbert?

RRRING RRRING

Hello? . . . Yes . . . Chambers speaking . . . Oh, yes sir . . . Right . . . right . . . you'll keep in touch? . . . Good!

Well, that's that . . . There are police check-points on all the roads in this area . . . they won't escape us . . . Never fear . . .

Diabolo! . . . The police!

PAAAARP

The swine!

Yes . . . Police patrol at Wallinghead reporting . . . The car has just passed here at high speed, proceeding in a south-westerly direction . . . You've got a road-block in position? . . . Good . . .

Look, there's a car coming . . .

Excuse me, sir, but have you seen a black saloon car on the road?

A black saloon? . . . I don't think so . . . I wasn't paying much attention.

Here comes another . . .

25707

A black Opel saloon? . . . No . . . no . . . I don't recall seeing one . . .

Carry on,   sir.

Odd! . . . Where can they have gone?

We'll soon find out! . . . We'll make a reconnaissance.

Kidnapping Calculus! . . . Band of thugs! . . . Why pick on Calculus? . . . And why did he have to go walking in the garden, anyway?

Ah! Now we'll know.

What? You haven't seen them? . . . But it's ages since they went past us! . . . They almost ran us down!

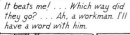

It beats me! . . . Which way did they go? . . . Ah, a workman. I'll have a word with him.

A black car? . . . I don't know if it's the one you're looking for, but a car turned down there about three-quarters of an hour ago . . . to the right, into the wood.

Good. Thanks.

!

RRRING
RRRING

Hello, yes . . . yes . . . Well? . . . You've found it? That's splen . . . What? . . . Empty!

Quick, Captain, we'll hop in the car . . . We might learn something over there . . .

Nest of rattlesnakes! . . . Pirates! . . . Bashi-bazouks!

You found it here? Abandoned, like this?

Yes. But the occupants won't get far. The whole area is cordoned off, and we're beating the wood . . . The man they've kidnapped - is he   a friend of yours?

It's Calculus, you poor loon! . . . Calculus! . . . The salt of the earth . . . with a heart of gold! He's been kidnapped by those devils! . . . Why? I ask you . . . Thundering typhoons, d'you know why?

Me? . . . No.

Well, Sherlock Holmes . . . Have you found anything?

Could be . . .

I say, officer, you were at one of the road-blocks weren't you? So you should have seen a large fawn-coloured car go by . . .

A large fawn   car? Just let me think . . .

Good heavens, you're right! A fawn car did pass us . . . A saloon . . . I stopped it myself.

You didn't think of taking the number?

No . . . why should I? . . . But wait a bit . . . The driver looked like a foreigner: Spanish, or South American, or something like that . . . Fattish, sun-tanned, black moustache and side-boards, horn-rimmed glasses . . .

And the others? . . . There were some others, I suppose?

Yes, there was someone sitting beside him . . . Another foreigner, I'd say: dark hair, bony face, hooked nose, thin lips . . . I think there were two other men in the back, but I only caught a glimpse of them.

Good! . . . Well, you can call off the beaters . . . It's a waste of time. The kidnappers are far away.

Oh, yes? How do you know that?

How do I know? . . . Look at these tracks . . . Here are the tyre-marks of the Opel. But here are some others, different tyres. Dunlop I'd say: the tyres of the car that was waiting for the Opel.

Blistering barnacles, you're right! But how did you guess that it was fawn-coloured?

Look here . . .

Specks of fawn paint . . . The lane is narrow. In turning, one of the wings of the car scraped against this tree, leaving traces of paint.

The crooks! So they switched cars!

Come on, we must pass all this on to the police at once. Perhaps they'll be able to catch them further on . . .

The next morning . . .

Let's see . . . Ah, here . . .

"The car used by the kidnappers is a large fawn saloon . . ." Good . . . "The occupants are believed to be of South American origin . . ." That's right . . . "Anyone who can give any information is asked to get in touch with the nearest police station immediately."

Oh well, there's still some hope left . . .

RRRING RRRING

Hello, this is Thomson . . . Yes, without a P . . . I say, there's something very queer going on at the hospital where the seven explorers are detained . . . I think you'd better slip round there . . .

It's really serious? . . . I can't believe it! . . . What? . . . Yes . . . Of course . . . Don't worry, I'll go round at once.

HOSPITAL

Yes, it is most extraordinary. Every day, at the same time, the seven patients go into some sort of trance . . . It's quite inexplicable . . . Look, it's almost time for their seizure now . . . You'll see what I mean . . .

Some of the leading consultants in this field are in the ward now, waiting for the symptoms to appear.

Here are the patients. You'll see . . .

They all look quite peaceful to me.

For the time being. But wait, it'll soon begin . . . There!

HOSPITAL

It's certainly very peculiar.

But what possible connection can there be between all this and the kidnapping of Calculus?

The next day . . .

Good afternoon, Nestor. How is the Captain?

Oh sir, he's aged ten years since this trouble began . . . And you, sir? Have you any news?

None Nestor. Poor Professor Calculus has vanished into thin air.

Oh dear, oh dear! The master will be so disappointed.

He's there, sir.

Hello, Captain.

Ah, Tintin! Hello . . . Well, what about Calculus? Anything new?

Nothing at all, I'm afraid.

Thundering typhoons.

WOOAH GRRR FFFH

Snowy! . . . Here, Snowy!

Wooah! Wooah!

RRRRING

Hello . . . Yes, it's me . . . Who's that? . . . Oh? . . . Well, what news? . . . What?!

116

What did you say? . . . At a garage . . . Two days ago! . . . Then they went off again? . . . Ten thousand thundering typhoons!

⁉

Hello! . . . Hello! . . .

Once and for all, will you leave that cat alone!

Blistering barnacles, let's go!

?

I say, Captain, what's going on?

Captain! . . . Captain, where are you going?

BANG

Hey, Captain!

BANG

Captain! . . . Captain!

Sir! Sir! It's me, Nestor . . . There's no answer . . . I wonder if I dare presume to . . .

Of course, Nestor: go on! Look through the keyhole . . .

Can you see anything?

Nothing, I . . .

?

Let's go!

Let's go where, Captain?

Just time for a noggin – one for the road, and we're off!

Wooah! Wooah!

!

Snowy! Come here, Snowy!

Wooah! Wooah!

!

?!?

Snowy, Snowy, now what have you done?

CLICK

Snowy! . . . Here, Snowy!

Stop, Snowy! Stop!

Meanwhile . . .

Just one more tot . . . the last . . .

My poor, poor friend. What has become of you?

Here's to you, Cuthbert old chap. We'll find you, I promise - dead or alive.

As I've told you before - more to the west!

And now perhaps you'll be kind enough to behave yourself. Otherwise it's a muzzle and lead . . . understand?

What is it now? Oh, you're thirsty? All right, go on.

Mm-m-m-m! This is what I call water!

And now, Captain, will you please tell me where we're going?

To Westermouth.

The police rang me . . . The fawn car was seen near there two days ago by a garage-hand. They stopped at a pump for petrol, then left, heading towards the docks. Undoubtedly the kidnappers have boarded a ship with Calculus . . . And so will we . . .

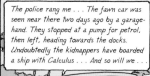

. . . by thunder, and snatch him from the grasp of those iconoclasts, those vampires, those . . . And just think: Westermouth, docks, jetties, the ocean, the sea-breezes whipping the spray in your face . . .

As for the spray, Captain, you've got your wish!

Blistering barnacles! . . . Quick, the hood, or we'll be drenched!

What's up?

Thundering typhoons, it's stuck! . . . Something's caught up . . . I'll try to do it from inside the car . . .

Billions of blistering barnacles!

That's got it!

About time too!

Thundering typhoons! I'm soaked!

Everything happens to me!

Oh, well, at least I'm a bit drier now . . .

Gangsters! . . . Road-hogs! . . . Mountebanks! Steamrollers! . . . Nyctalops! . . . Parasites!

Sea-gherkins! . . . Pock-marks! Cannibals!

Come on, Captain; hurry up, or we'll never get there.

As soon as we get to Westermouth tomorrow, we'll go straight to the police; they'll put us in the picture . . .

Early next morning . . .

I'm sorry, there's nothing fresh . . . It was a fawn car all right; but was it the one containing your friend? It was seen heading for Westermouth . . . and since then, nothing . . . it has simply vanished.

The search is continuing, that's all I can tell you. But in my opinion, there's very little chance . . . Excuse me . . .

Hello? . . . Yes, this is Inspector Jackson . . . Yes . . . Again? . . . What? . . . Where? . . . In one of the docks? . . . Well I'm . . . !! There's no mistake about it? . . . Excellent!

Well, gentlemen, you're in luck! The fawn car has just been recovered from one of the docks. If you'd like to come with me, we'll go and have a look.

Thanks very much!

It was a trawler, coming in. She struck an obstacle, so we dragged the dock . . . And there you are.

Is there any means of identification? . . . Number plate? . . . Licence? . . . Engine number?

Nothing at all, sir. There are no number plates, and the engine and chassis numbers have been filed off. It's a mass-produced car, so there isn't much chance of ever finding out . . .

Yes, I see . . .

Anyway, we can be certain of one thing: whoever kidnapped Professor Calculus embarked here, having first tried to get rid of the car by dumping it in the dock.

Yes . . . yes . . . perhaps . . .

We must act at once: we'll radio a description of your friend to all the ships that have sailed from Westermouth since the twelfth . . . Then we'll see what happens.

Thanks, Inspector – and you'll let us know how things are going?

All things considered, we're not much further on.

I know.

Hello, she's leaving for South America . . . and the kidnappers could be aboard . . . with poor Calculus!

Great snakes! . . . That looks like . . . Yes, it is!

Hey! . . . Who are you?

Police!

Hello, General!

Ay Dios de mi vida! ... Tintin! Amigo mio!

Nice to see you, General. Are you off on tour?

On tour? ... Caramba! ... I go home to my own country. Music-hall, for me is finished ... No more partner.

No partner? ... What's happened to Chiquito?

Gone! ... Disappeared! ... Four days ago ... I not blame him ... Before we come to Europe he say he leave me one day: not to worry, not to look for him ... And, it is so.

Four days ago? ... Then he disappeared on the twelfth ... well, well. Tell me: is Chiquito a real Indian?

Is Chiquito a real Indian? Santa Madre de Dios! ... He is one of last descendants of los Incas!

What? A descendant of the Incas? ... You're sure of that?

Absolutely sure! He is pure-blooded Quichua Indian ... Chiquito is just stage name. His real name is Rupac Inca Huaco.

Rupac Inca Huaco? ... I wonder ... The thin man beside the driver, in the fawn car ...

The fawn car?

Have you ever seen Chiquito with a rather fat man with a small black moustache and horn-rimmed glasses? ... Perhaps a Peruvian ...

Never. He never see anybody, never speak to anybody except me ...

TOOOOOT

Caramba! I must go now ... Adios, amigo mio ... We meet again, perhaps!

Good luck!

All aboard!

Well, who did you see over there?

General Alcazar.

He told me two very odd things ... First his partner Chiquito disappeared on the twelfth ... That was the night Professor Tarragon was attacked, and the mummy's jewels stolen. The next day Calculus was kidnapped.

Secondly, Chiquito's real name is Rupac Inca Huaco, and he's a descendant of the Incas!

What?

Strange coincidences, eh? Very strange ... What do you say to that?

Hey! ... Whoa! ... Stop! ...

?

Blistering barnacles, put me down! Put me down at once!

Numbskulls! ... Hi-jackers!

But Captain, I ...

Kleptomaniacs! ... Body-snatchers!

Come on, let's go, Captain.

We'll go and tell the Inspector what General Alcazar had to say ... about the mystery of Chiquito.

There, I've made a note of it all ... We'll try to track down this Chiquito fellow ... It could be that he's mixed up in this business somewhere ... Anyway, I'll let you know how things are going.

So that's that. Now what shall we do, Captain?

I haven't a notion.

Wait a minute! I've got an idea ...

Well?

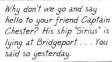
Why don't we go and say hello to your friend Captain Chester? His ship "Sirius" is lying at Bridgeport . . . You said so yesterday.

Good for you! Let's go . . .

Now where's the "Sirius"? Chester told me he was berthed at Quay No. 18 . . . We'll have to ask someone . . .

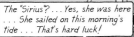
The "Sirius"? . . . Yes, she was here . . . She sailed on this morning's tide . . . That's hard luck!

Hard luck! It certainly is! . . . If only we had some news of Calculus . . . the smallest clue . . .

Hard luck!

Yeoww!

It's the classic joke! . . . A stone hidden under an old hat!

Oww! Yoww!! Yeeoww!!!

There, Captain, look! Those boys . . . they did it!

Vagabonds! . . . Hooligans! . . . Iconoclasts! . . .

Captain! Captain! Don't do that! It's terribly dangerous!

Yes, you're right . . . Anyway, they're well out of range!

Still, if I get my hands on the young jackanapes they won't forget Captain Haddock in a hurry!

THUD
SPLOSH
?

Whew, that was a near thing!

Hello, Snowy. What have you got there? . . . A hat?

Goodness, it's the same one . . . The one the Captain kicked.

There . . . And leave the dirty thing alone!

Here, Snowy! Come here! And put that hat down!

Why can't you do as you're told?

We'll put a stop to your little game . . .

Now! . . . At least you won't go in there after it!

?

Come along, Snowy! . . . Here!

Wooah! Wooah!

SPLASH

!

!

Oh, so you're trying to make a fool of me, are you?

Donkey! What do you want me to do with that hat? Wear it?

Then I'd look like . . . Crumbs! . . . No, it's impossible!

!

Captain! . . . Captain! . . . I've got Calculus's hat!

Old Cuthbert's little round hat! . . . That's why Snowy insisted on retrieving it . . . Look at the initials!

C.C.: Cuthbert Calculus! . . . But then . . .

Calculus wasn't taken aboard at Westermouth. It was here at Bridgeport . . . But what ship? . . . And what was her destination? . . . That's what we need to know.

But how can we find out?

I've got it! We must try to find those two lads who played the trick with the hat.

Yes! I'll teach the young pirates a thing or two!

On the contrary, Captain, you'll be very nice to them . . . After all, thanks to them we found the hat . . . and we want them to tell us how they came by it themselves.

Oh, yes . . .

Good old Snowy; because of you we've made a wonderful discovery . . . Now we want you to help us again . . . We must find those two scamps . . . you ran after them remember?

An hour later . . .

?

Hey, what's bitten you?

Hello there!

!

Don't worry, we're not looking for trouble. We just want to know where you found this hat?

That hat? . . . We were down in No. 17 shed this morning . . . where the crates were stacked for loading aboard . . .

. . . the "Black Cat" . . . When they lifted one of the crates out of the shed, I saw the hat underneath, all flattened out . . . Honestly, it wasn't my idea to play that trick . . . it was my friend . . .

Well, your friend had a jolly good idea . . . Didn't he, Captain?

Now, Captain, to the harbour master's office. We'll ask them when the packing-cases came into the warehouse.

The cases? . . . They arrived on the fourteenth, by rail . . . This morning they were loaded aboard the "Black Cat".

And the night before they arrived, was a ship berthed opposite shed No. 17?

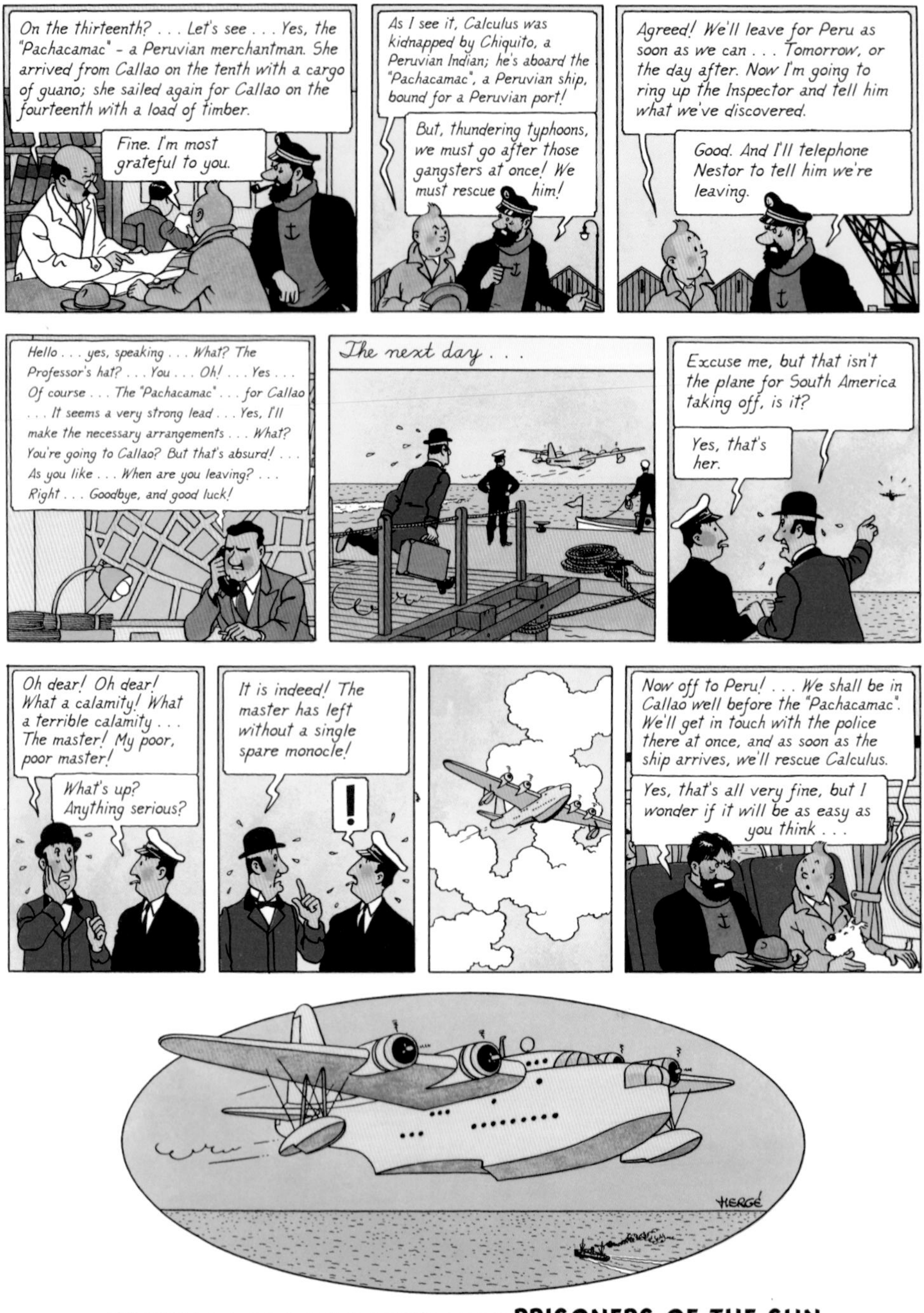

On the thirteenth? . . . Let's see . . . Yes, the "Pachacamac" – a Peruvian merchantman. She arrived from Callao on the tenth with a cargo of guano; she sailed again for Callao on the fourteenth with a load of timber.
Fine. I'm most grateful to you.
As I see it, Calculus was kidnapped by Chiquito, a Peruvian Indian; he's aboard the "Pachacamac", a Peruvian ship, bound for a Peruvian port!
But, thundering typhoons, we must go after those gangsters at once! We must rescue him!
Agreed! We'll leave for Peru as soon as we can . . . Tomorrow, or the day after. Now I'm going to ring up the Inspector and tell him what we've discovered.
Good. And I'll telephone Nestor to tell him we're leaving.
Hello . . . yes, speaking . . . What? The Professor's hat? . . . You . . . Oh! . . . Yes . . . Of course . . . The "Pachacamac" . . . for Callao . . . It seems a very strong lead . . . Yes, I'll make the necessary arrangements . . . What? You're going to Callao? But that's absurd! . . . As you like . . . When are you leaving? . . . Right . . . Goodbye, and good luck!
The next day . . .
Excuse me, but that isn't the plane for South America taking off, is it?
Yes, that's her.
Oh dear! Oh dear! What a calamity! What a terrible calamity . . . The master! My poor, poor master!
What's up? Anything serious?
It is indeed! The master has left without a single spare monocle!
!
Now off to Peru! . . . We shall be in Callao well before the "Pachacamac". We'll get in touch with the police there at once, and as soon as the ship arrives, we'll rescue Calculus.
Yes, that's all very fine, but I wonder if it will be as easy as you think . . .
HERGÉ

What will happen in Peru? You will find out in **PRISONERS OF THE SUN**

HERGÉ
★
THE ADVENTURES OF
TINTIN
★

PRISONERS OF
THE SUN

LITTLE, BROWN AND COMPANY
New York   Boston

PRISONERS OF THE SUN

At Police Headquarters in Callao, Peru . . .

SOUTH AMERICA

Callao

PACIFIC OCEAN

ATLANTIC OCEAN

Haddock, a retired ship's captain, and Tintin, the reporter? Oh, yes, Interpol warned me they'd be coming. Send them in.

As I understand it, this is the situation: your friend Professor Calculus has been kidnapped, and you have good reason to believe he's aboard the cargo ship "Pachacamac" - due to arrive in Callao any day now. Am I right?*

Absolutely.

Well, gentlemen, as soon as the "Pachacamac" comes into port we will search the ship. If your friend really is aboard, then he will be restored to you immediately. Now, we can only . . .

Look down there; an Indian running away! . . . Someone was spying on us!

Surely you're mistaken . . .

No, no, I saw him quite clearly; an Indian, peering through the railings. He disappeared behind those bushes.

Bah! What does it matter? There was nothing confidential in what we said.

Why not forget the whole incident . . . and allow me to offer you a glass of pisco? It's our national drink. Come, here's to the safe return of your friend Calculus.

* See The Seven Crystal Balls

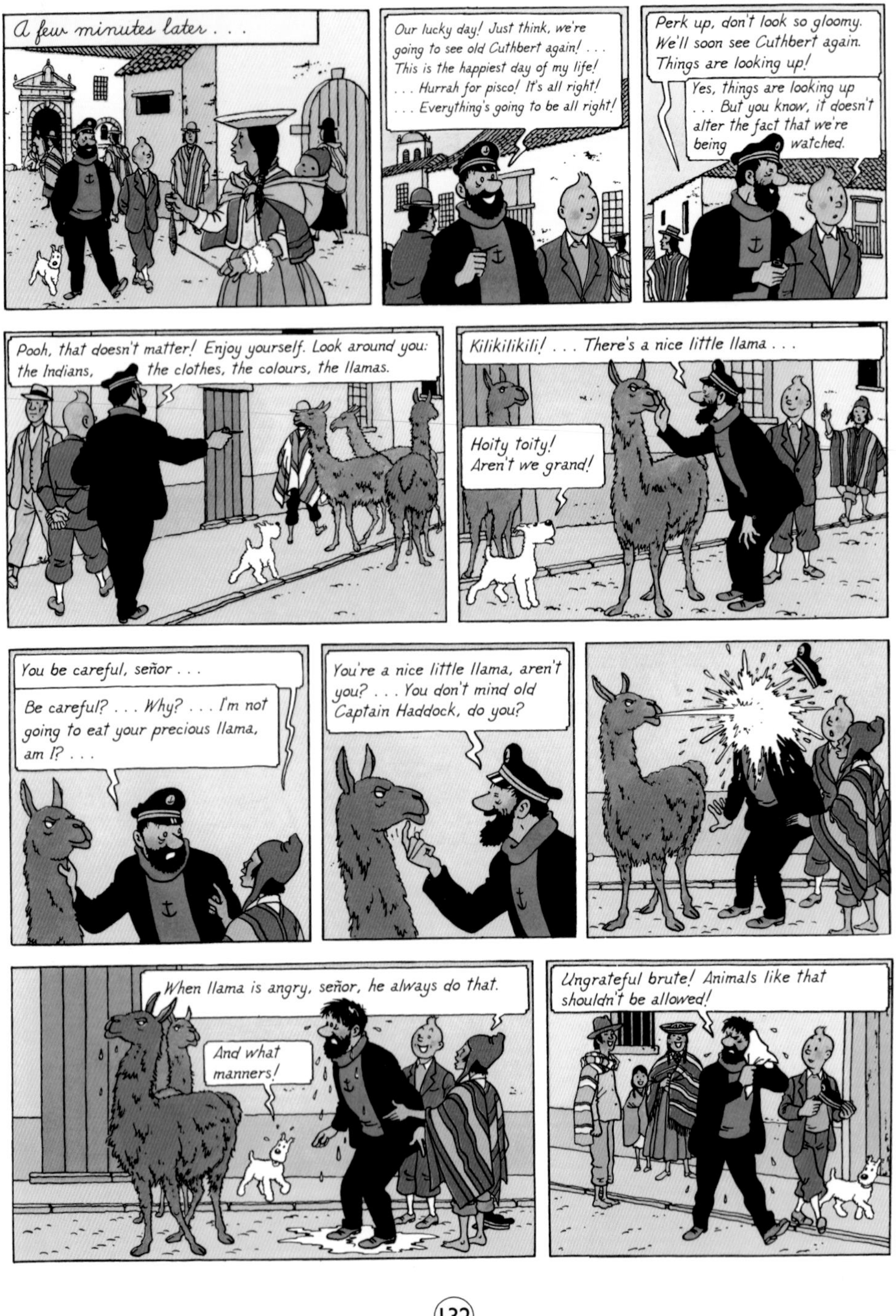
A few minutes later . . .
Our lucky day! Just think, we're going to see old Cuthbert again! . . . This is the happiest day of my life! . . . Hurrah for pisco! It's all right! . . . Everything's going to be all right!
Perk up, don't look so gloomy. We'll soon see Cuthbert again. Things are looking up!
Yes, things are looking up . . . But you know, it doesn't alter the fact that we're being watched.
Pooh, that doesn't matter! Enjoy yourself. Look around you: the Indians, the clothes, the colours, the llamas.
Kilikilikili! . . . There's a nice little llama . . .
Hoity toity! Aren't we grand!
You be careful, señor . . .
Be careful? . . . Why? . . . I'm not going to eat your precious llama, am I? . . .
You're a nice little llama, aren't you? . . . You don't mind old Captain Haddock, do you?
When llama is angry, señor, he always do that.
And what manners!
Ungrateful brute! Animals like that shouldn't be allowed!

Perk up, Captain, don't look so gloomy. Remember, you said it yourself just now: things are looking up, we're going to see old Cuthbert again.

Hotel Cristobal Colon. Bueno . . .

The next morning . . .

RRRING

Hello . . . yes, Tintin speaking . . . Good morning, señor Chief Inspector . . . What? . . . The "Pachacamac" is in sight? . . . Fine! . . . Quay No. 24 . . . We'll be there right away.

A few minutes later . . .

There's the Chief Inspector with his men, down on the quayside . . .

But . . . I must be seeing things . . . Look!

Thomson and Thompson! What are those nitwits doing here?

You asked about your friends . . . well, here they come.

What a coincidence!

Not at all. These gentlemen were sent out by the C.I.D. to help in the search for your friend.

Now for the "Pachacamac". Where is she?

Out there, to the left of that little tug with the red funnel . . .

Ah, now I've got it . . . There she is . . . it's her all right . . . "Pachacamac" . . . let's hope old Calculus is on board!

Thundering typhoons!

?

Blistering barnacles! The "Pachacamac" is running up the yellow flag and a yellow and blue pennant: infectious disease on board!

Goodness gracious! And we've got to go on board to search the ship.

It's out of the question till the port health authorities have cleared her . . .

There goes the doctor's launch now, heading for the "Pachacamac" . . .

Well . . . we can only wait until they've finished.

?

I say, Captain, just what is that stuff, guano?

Guano? . . . Er . . . How shall I put it? . . .

PLOP

Guano? . . . Well, there's a free sample!

So you think that's funny, eh? . . . A brand new hat! . . . Ha ha; very amusing.

PLOP

Captain . . . The "Pachacamac" is hoisting more flags!

!

Billions of blue bubonic barnacles! She'll be quarantined!

Are they celebrating the Captain's birthday?

Putting a ship in quarantine, you landlubber, means keeping her in isolation for some time, to avoid risk of infection.

There's the launch coming back . . .

Well, doctor?

Two cases of yellow fever on board. I've ordered three weeks' quarantine.

You heard? . . . I'm terribly sorry about that . . . You'll just have to be patient.

Yes . . . obviously. Tell me, isn't that doctor an Indian?

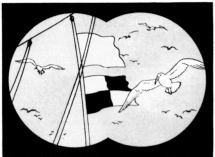

A Quichua, as a matter of fact. Why?

Oh, no reason. I just wondered.

A little later . . .

Thundering typhoons! Three weeks . . . Three weeks without knowing whether Calculus is even aboard that blistering bathtub!

There's no question of waiting three weeks . . . We're going to find out tonight!

What do you mean, tonight?

Tonight I shall go aboard the "Pachacamac".

Tonight? . . . You? . . . What about the yellow fever, stupid? . . . Have you forgotten?

Captain, I'll bet anything you like that every man aboard the "Pachacamac" is as fit as you and me.

But thundering typhoons, the doctor definitely said . . .

The doctor is an Indian, Captain . . . a Quichua Indian . . . Doesn't that mean anything to you? . . .

Night has fallen . . .

Stop! We won't go any further . . .
We might be seen.

Right . . . You're quite sure?
I told you, there are sharks
around here . . .

Nuts to the sharks! Anyway,
they should be fast asleep at
this hour, like everyone else!

Just as you
like . . .

There . . . You know the drill, don't you:
if I'm not back in a couple of hours,
inform the police . . . Goodbye, Captain.
And you be a good boy, Snowy.

Good luck,
Tintin.

Thundering typhoons! . . .
There's no stopping him!

Now comes the most
difficult part . . .

¿Qué pasa,
ahí abajo? . . .

¿Quien es?

Crumbs! Somebody else!

There's nothing for it . . . into this cabin, quick!

All's well, he didn't see me . . . He's going past . . .

¿Qué ha pasado, Chiquito? . . .

No es nada, debe de ser el gato . . .

Fine! They think it's a cat!

He's going back into his cabin . . . He's shut the door . . . Whew! . . .

ZZZZZ
ZZZZZ

Someone's in that bunk. I must get out of here!

Excuse me . . . A little further to the west!

There's only one person in the world who talks like that . . . and that is . . .

Cuthbert Calculus!

Professor! . . . Professor! . . . Wake up! . . . It's me, Tintin! Please, please wake up!

Nothing I can do . . . He's obviously been drugged!

Hello, whatever's that? . . . What's he got there, round his wrist?

The bracelet from the mummy!

Si, the bracelet of Rascar Capac!

Why, it's . . . it's Chiquito!

Si, Chiquito.

What do you want with poor Calculus?

He has committed sacrilege: he has put on the Inca bracelet! He must die! . . . As for you, you are a prisoner. I will decide later what your fate will be.

Alonzo!

You there! Stop!

Great snakes, another!

Quick, over the side!

Little devil, you will pay for this!

Thundering typhoons! . . . Those guano-gatherers are murdering Tintin!

Iconoclasts! . . . Pirates! . . . Just a few more strokes . . .

. . . and someone's going to get it in the neck!

?

Wooah! Wooah!

Blistering barnacles!

Wooah! Wooah!

And you shut up, you sealion, you!

Ah, there's Tintin.

BANG

BANG

Wooah!

Quick, climb aboard . . . Not hurt, are you?

No, not a scratch . . . But let's get out of here, fast!

Calculus is on board, Captain, I saw him. They're going to put him to death. They say he committed sacrilege by wearing an Inca bracelet.

Back to the shore! We must get reinforcements!

You dash back to the town and alert the police. I'll stay here and keep watch.

No sleep for us tonight, Snowy.

I might've guessed!

All quiet. But after what's happened they're bound to make a move . . . Yes, they're launching a boat. I hope the Captain gets help quickly . . .

A 'phone box, at last!

Hello . . . Yes . . . Police Headquarters . . . What? . . . You want to talk to the señor Chief Inspector? . . . At this hour? Have you gone crazy? . . . The señor Chief Inspector is asleep!

Thundering typhoons, I know that! If he wasn't asleep you wouldn't have to wake him up! . . . Tell him it's very, very urgent!

You're breaking my heart! . . . Look, it may be urgent, but nobody wakes the señor Chief Inspector at four a.m.!

But you must wake him, I tell you, it's . . . Hello . . . Hello . . . Hello . . . The blistering blundering bird-brain, he's hung up!

Meanwhile . . .
The boat's getting nearer . . . Come on, Snowy, but don't show yourself. We're going to take a closer look at them . . .

I've got an idea . . . I'll ring up the Thompsons . . . Four, two, eight . . . That's it . . .

That sounds like the telephone.

To be precise: the telephone.

Great snakes . . . They're carrying Calculus ashore!

RRRRING

Are you going to answer it?

Me? . . . Certainly not . . . how can I? I'm asleep!

Taking their time, the baboons!

RRRRING

You can't be asleep, you're talking to me!

You know very well that I talk in my sleep!

Blue blistering barnacles! I can't stand here all night!

Very well, I'll go. But next time, it's your turn!

Hello? . . . Hello, Thomson? . . . And about time too! . . . This is Captain Haddock . . .

What? . . . Who? . . . Oh, yes, Captain Haddock . . . I . . . What? . . . Calculus? . . . Where? . . . Yes . . . Right . . . We'll come at once . . .

Half an hour later . . .
Nearly two hours since I left him . . . I hope he's all right.

There's our boat . . . I left Tintin here . . . But where is he?

Tintin! Hi, Tintin!

Tintin!

No use shouting ourselves hoarse. Tintin's gone. We must examine the beach; we ought to pick up his tracks quite quickly.

It's like looking for a needle in a haystack.

To be precise: we look like needles in a haystack.

Here, look at this! Footprints!

And others here. Look, there were several men, with horses . . . no, llamas . . . See these marks in the sand . . .

Come on. This way . . . it's plain sailing . . .

The footprints stop at the road . . . Still, no matter, it's obvious they kept going in the same direction.

Just a minute . . . What if it's a trick . . . Supposing they went in the opposite direction?

Quite right! . . . I submit that half of us should go one way, and half the other.

What a brilliant idea! There are three of us: half of three is one and a half . . .

Great Scotland Yard! You're right! What can we do?

You two go your way, and I'll go mine . . . And we'll see which of us finds Tintin . . . Goodbye . . . And keep your eyes open!

Don't worry, they're wide open!

To be precise: they're . . .

BLIND CORNER!

Many hours later . . .

Here, boy . . . Have you met anyone along this road – a young European, with a white dog?

?

Yes . . . and I've met him before!

Tintin! . . . You young rascal, you had me properly fooled! . . . Honestly, I'd never have recognised you . . . But why the disguise?

Come along . . . I'll explain.

Shortly after you left they brought Calculus ashore. They had accomplices waiting on the beach. They lifted Calculus on to a llama and led him away. I followed at a distance, making sure they didn't spot me . . .

We came to Santa Clara, a small town. I hastily bought this cap and poncho in the market, so I was able to get close to them at the station and see them buy tickets to Jauga . . .

What did they do with Calculus?

Obviously they'd drugged him; he followed them like a sleep-walker . . . Then the train left – without me, alas: I hadn't enough money for a ticket. After that I retraced my steps, hoping to find you . . .

Thundering typhoons! . . . The gangsters! Going off with Calculus! . . . But we'll catch the next train . . .

Of course! But unfortunately the train only runs every other day.

But why are you by yourself? Where are the police? Didn't you telephone them?

Still in bed . . . And the Thompsons are hot on your trail, somewhere . . .

Two days later . . .

Our seats are in the last coach, aren't they?

Si, señor.

Lucky we arrived in good time: the train's going to be crammed.

No, no - it is impossible . . . You ask too much . . . I cannot . . .

It is his order - and you know what happens to those who disobey him . . .

Half an hour later . . .

TOOOT

We're off . . . How odd: all that crowd of passengers, but not a soul has got into our compartment.

RESERVED

Have a good trip, señores!

The train steams on for several hours . . .

Excuse me: I'll be back in a minute.

It's a funny thing . . . D'you know, we're absolutely alone in this carriage.

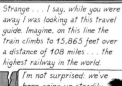

Strange . . . I say, while you were away I was looking at this travel guide. Imagine, on this line the train climbs to 15,865 feet over a distance of 108 miles . . . the highest railway in the world.

I'm not surprised: we've been going up steadily.

Hello, we're slowing down . . . I expect we're coming to a station.

Captain, get out, quick! The coupling has broken and our coach is running away!

Quick, jump!

My turn . . . Now for it!

Great snakes! I've forgotten . . .

Billions of blistering barnacles! Why doesn't he jump?

Crumbs! A tunnel! Snowy! Snowy!

Oww!

Snowy! . . . Snowy!

He's still asleep!

Come, quick!

?

It's too late! We'd be killed!

The emergency brake! I didn't think . . .

Our last chance! . . . Here goes!

!

Sabotage! . . . Now I see the whole thing!

What can I do now? . . .

A viaduct . . . A river . . . Snowy, old boy, this is it.

Careful . . . Wait for it!

Tintin! . . .
Where is Tintin?

?

CRASH CRACK

Oh, look! . . . The coach has gone over the edge . . . We just made it!

!

We can thank our lucky stars we got out of that, Snowy!

You're telling me!

First let's get dry . . . Then we must try to find the Captain . . .

Come on Snowy, one last effort, you're nearly there.

Now, on our way. We must join up with the Captain.

Still no sign . . . Was he hurt when he jumped?

What has become of him?

Hooray!

Hooray!

Safe and sound! What an escape!

TOOOOT

Hey, stop! . . . Arrêtez! . . . Whoa!

You were in the runaway coach? You were able to jump in time? . . . How fortunate!

I am in charge at the next station . . . When the train arrived we found a coach missing . . . I was most upset: it is the first accident we have had on this line . . .

Accident? . . . You mean attempted murder!

Attempted murder? . . . But that is impossible!

All the same, it's true. But don't let's waste time. We were going to Jauga . . . Will you take us there?

Some hours later, in Jauga . . .

A short man, you say, with a little black beard, and glasses? . . . Yes, I think . . . Wait . . . He was accompanied by some Indians, wasn't he?

You mean he was a prisoner of the Indians. Our friend has been kidnapped.

Kidnapped by the Indians? . . . I . . . er . . . No, he wasn't the man you're looking for . . . The one I'm talking about seemed to be following the Indians quite willingly.

Naturally; he'd been drugged.

You think so? . . . That is not very likely . . . But now I come to think of it, the man . . . Yes, the man I saw was tall, and fair . . . and clean-shaven.

But you told us yourself, just a moment ago . . .

I was mistaken, that's all . . . I am sorry I can be of no further assistance to you, gentlemen . . . The interview is closed!

Why that sudden change? . . . Curious . . . He seemed anxious not to be involved. Is he afraid of the Indians?

Only one thing to do: split up and question some of the locals.

Right! . . . We'll meet outside the station in an hour.

A short man, with a little beard, and wearing glasses . . . you see him?

No sé!

Short man . . . little beard . . . glasses . . . You see him?

No sé!

You see him?

No sé!

No sé! No sé! . . . They're the only words they know, the stubborn South American centipedes!

? Por favor, kind señor.

No sé! ?

Meanwhile . . .

No sé! No sé! . . . That's a fat lot of good! They must know something . . . But they seem to be afraid . . .

Oh well, I'll ask that young orange-seller . . .

No sé I'll bet!

Here comes Zorrino . . . Hold everything: this'll be rich!

Ha! ha! ha! ha!

Ha! ha! ha! ha!

Ha! ha! ha!

Ha! ha! ha!

Lost something, sonny boy?

Aaaaah!

Brute!

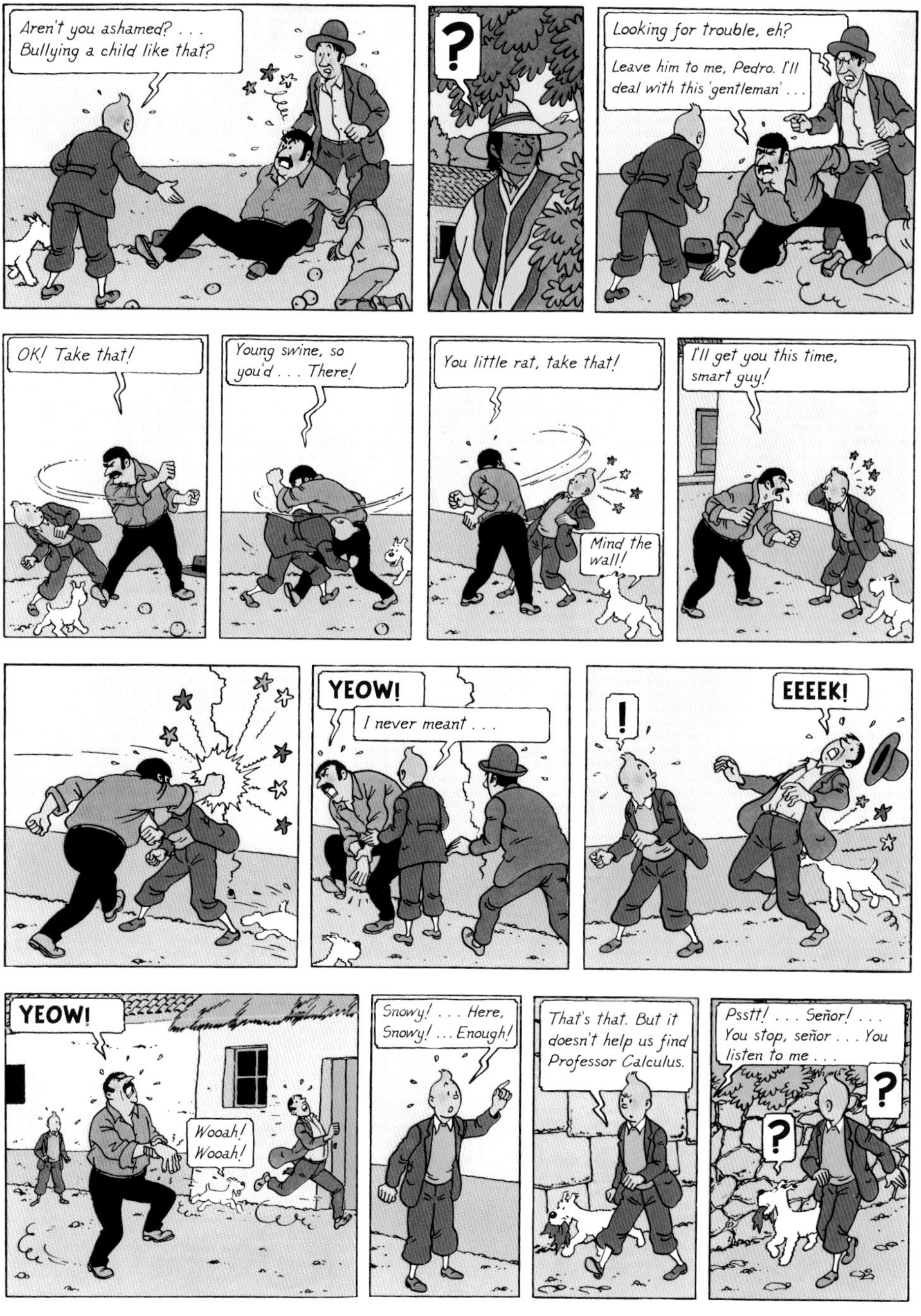
Aren't you ashamed? . . . Bullying a child like that?
?
Looking for trouble, eh?
Leave him to me, Pedro. I'll deal with this 'gentleman' . . .
OK! Take that!
Young swine, so you'd . . . There!
You little rat, take that!
Mind the wall!
I'll get you this time, smart guy!
YEOW!
I never meant . . .
!
EEEEK!
YEOW!
Wooah! Wooah!
Snowy! . . . Here, Snowy! . . . Enough!
That's that. But it doesn't help us find Professor Calculus.
Psstt! . . . Señor! . . . You stop, señor . . . You listen to me . . .
?
?

You not look this way . . . You tie up your shoelace . . .

I know where your friend is prisoner . . . You buy guns and come tomorrow, at sunrise, to Bridge of the Inca . . . You understand? . . . Bridge of the Inca . . . You go now.

Fantastic! A guide straight out of the blue!

What if it's a trap?

You listen to me, señor . . .

?

?

I see you go to help Indian boy . . . You are good . . . You are brave . . .

Er . . . I . . . Who are you?

I speak wise words . . . You not go in search of your friend, otherwise you meet many dangers.

How do you know?

I know, señor . . . You remember train that ran away . . . You have good luck that time . . . But you not always have good luck . . . You listen to me: you not go . . .

I can't abandon my friend – but thank you, anyway.

That is very foolish choice . . . You still go, then take this . . . Very good, help you in danger . . .

A little medal . . . a talisman. What do you . . .

!

Next morning, at dawn . . .

Blistering barnacles, why doesn't he show up, this guide of yours?

Pssst . . . Psssst!

!

!

Quick, señores! . . . You come now!

Careful, be on your guard!

(150)

Why, it's the little orange-seller . . . the one I told you about.

So it was you . . .

Yes, I talk to you yesterday, from behind wall . . . If Indians see me speak to you, they kill me at once . . . You come now . . .

You wait for me on other side of bridge . . . I come back quick.

Where's he off to?

I don't know. He told us to wait.

Thundering typhoons! Llamas!

To carry supplies, señores . . . Journey very long!

This is too much! . . . If you think I'm travelling around with this pair of perambulating fire-pumps, you're very much mistaken!

Llamas very gentle, señor. You not be afraid.

Afraid? . . . Me? . . . Afraid of these moth-eaten imitation camels? . . . I've only got to look them straight in the eye and they'll be eating out of my hand!

Like that . . . there!

YEEEEOW!

You miserable iconoclast!

You not hit him, señor.

When llama angry . . .

Blistering barnacles, I know! . . . When llama angry, he always do that!

Come on, we've wasted enough time . . . Are we ready, er . . .? Look, we don't even know your name . . .

Zorrino, señor.

Now look, Zorrino: where is our friend? . . . And why would none of the Indians tell us, though they all seemed to know what had happened to him?

He is prisoner in Temple of the Sun . . . But no one tell . . . all afraid.

Afraid? Of whom?

Afraid of Inca, señor. Vengeance of Inca terrible when Indian tell white man what white man must not know.

The Inca? . . . The Temple of the Sun? . . . An Inca, in these days? . . . It's unbelievable.

White men not know, señor. Only you know.

Thanks to you, Zorrino; but aren't you afraid of the Inca, too?

Alone, I afraid: with you, I not afraid!

That evening . . .

There is chulpa, señor, old Inca tomb. We spend night there, go on again in morning.

I'll stand the first watch. At about midnight I'll wake you, and you can take over.

Right.

Good night, Captain. And don't forget to wake me in good time.

Don't worry, I will . . . Sleep well, both of you.

Good night, Zorrino.

Good night, señor Tintin.

Amazing! An Inca plant in bloom!

Excuse me, señor Inca, but have you a licence for that gun?

A licence? . . . Sacrilege! Sacrilege! . . . The fire of heaven will strike you down!

Ugh! What a horrible nightmare! . . . It's just a ray of sunlight . . . But . . .

!

Good heavens, they let me sleep on . . . Captain! . . . I say, Captain! Ahoy there! . . .

Captain! . . . Captain! . . . Zorrino! . . .

. . . orrino!

. . . orrino!

Nothing . . . only the echo . . . What's become of them?

Having breakfast, I'll bet!

I don't like it: I'd better get my gun!

Great snakes! My gun: it's vanished!

Zorrino's cap; otherwise, not a trace of them . . .

WOOAH! WOOAH! WOOAH!

?

Quick! What has Snowy found?

WOOAH! WOOAH!

!

Captain! What in the world . . .

Cut the cackle and get me out of this before I go crazy!

?

Billions of blistering . . . I . . . I . . .

Hooray! Got it!

This miserable reptile has spent the night waltzing along my spine!

A lizard!

Careful!

Hey, look! It's dropping to bits!

WOOAH! WOOAH!

WOOAH! WOOAH!

Now, Captain, what happened?

Well, it was getting on towards midnight and I was walking up and down to keep warm. Suddenly a shadow rose up in front of me. There wasn't time to move a muscle before . . . Wham! . . . I felt a violent blow on the head . . . Next thing I knew, I was where you found me: tied up and gagged, with that lizard down my neck. What about Zorrino?

He's vanished, Captain, and so have the llamas, and our supplies. Much more serious, our guns have gone too!

Our guns? . . . The gangsters! . . . Bandits! . . . Filibusters! . . . Pirates! . . .

Thundering typhoons, what do we do now?

First of all, we must try to find Zorrino . . . Then tackle whoever's kidnapped him.

Snowy! . . .
Here, Snowy!

It's up to you now, Snowy . . .
We've got to find Zorrino.
Look, here's his cap . . .
Go on! . . . Seek him!

Come on! . . . After him!

WOOAH!
WOOAH!

Hey, not so fast, you
mountain goat, you!

Two hours later . . .

Stop! There
they are!

The path doubles back down
there . . . They'll pass directly
below us . . .

If we took a short cut down
the cliff we could surprise
them . . . Stay here, Snowy
. . . Come on, Captain!

We'll break our
necks, that's
a certainty!

Find some other way,
Captain: this is too steep.

Just in time! . . . Here they come! . . .
Careful, not a sound now . . .

?

HELP!

!

!

?

Help! he's fallen! . . . Ah, he's getting up . . . But they've caught him!

Here comes the last one . . . The others are out of sight . . . Now!

What's going on down there?

You tell, where is your friend? . . . Where Tintin?

No sé!

You know . . . You tell us; otherwise, you die.

Fiddle-de-dee to you . . . and abracadabra . . . and hocus pocus . . .

And fee-fi-fo-fum . . . And since you're so worried about my friend Tintin, take a look behind you!

? ?

All right, you thugs . . . Hands up!

Captain, will you disarm that Indian? . . . That's fine . . . Now if you'll untie Zorrino, I'll keep an eye on them . . .

Glad to see you, little'un.

All right?

Good! . . . That's disposed of them!

Señor!!

Hooray!

Come past me, Captain, while I cover you. You lot stay put!

Now then, get going down that path . . . fast! The first one who stops or comes back is a dead duck! . . . OK? . . . On your way . . . and take your pal with you!

I said fast!

Is no hurry . . .

BANG

CRACK

I think they've got the idea! Now I'll rejoin the others.

You see, Zorrino, we didn't abandon you.

I know you save me. Where is Snowy?

We left him higher up: he couldn't climb down . . . Look, there he is.

Hello, Snowy!

Wooah! Wooah!

Wooah! Wooah!

I've got a real bird's eye view!

Ooh! A condor!

Wooaaah!

Thundering typhoons!

Heavens! What can we do? . . . I daren't shoot . . .

WOOAH!

Snowy! Oh, poor, poor Snowy!

There . . . look . . . it's settled on a rock . . . Now or never! . . . Blistering barnacles, Tintin, be careful!

BANG

Hooray!

Quickly now! Ropes, and my scarf . . . I must go after Snowy . . .

You can't go up there!

You don't think I'd leave Snowy, Captain? . . . Injured, dying even . . .

Tintin, it's suicide, I tell you!

Snowy! . . . Snowy! . . . No answer!

Snowy! . . . Snowy!

Not a sound!

Oh, it's you? . . . I say, these birds certainly know how to treat a guest!

!?

Whew! What a relief! He's safe . . . for the moment at least. Now he's got to come down . . .

Why couldn't you have answered eh? . . . You're incorrigible! . . . Now, sit still!

This is it . . . down we go, gently now . . .

Oooh! I feel so giddy! . . . Why did I look?

Thundering typhoons! . . . Look, Zorrino! There! . . . Another condor! Quick, my rifle!

BANG

WHIUUW

! ! !

Missed, by thunder! . . . And I can't fire again now: the condor has got him!

Oh, Tintin! Tintin! . . . He'll be forced to let go!

It's all or nothing . . . I've no choice . . .

?

OOPS!

Blistering barnacles, what's going on? . . . He's hanging on to the condor's legs! . . . By thunder, what next?

Golly, a helicopter!

Pirate! . . . Doryphore! . . . Gobbledygook! Just wait till I get you to the taxidermist, you bald-headed budgerigar!

Saved!

A little later . . .

Blistering barnacles, what a country! . . . Is there no end to this mountainous menagerie?

Is it far now, Zorrino?

Far, señor, very far! . . . Still long journey to Temple of the Sun . . . Many days . . . Must cross high mountains, much snow . . .

Days go by . . .

One morning . . .

Narrow gully, señor . . . Is very dangerous . . . You not make noise, you not speak . . . otherwise avalanche come . . .

OK, little'un. We'll watch it.

Brrr! It's freezing! . . . You bet I'll catch a cold . . . There, what did I say? . . . Aaaah! . . . Aaaah! . . .

AAAAAAH . . .

TCHOOO

BRRROOM BRRROOM

An avalanche!

?

Quick! ... Behind this rock!

Whew! That's better ... It was a near thing ... Quick, I must dig Zorrino out!

Where llamas? ... And Captain?

I don't know, Zorrino ... Buried somewhere under the snow ... We must find them.

Captain! ... Captain!

Careful! ... You not shout!

Crumbs! You're right! ... Will it ...? No, nothing's moving now.

Wooah! Wooah!

!

The Captain! ... He's found the Captain!

Come on! To work! ... Where is he?

There!

No sign of life! ... We must get him out ... and quickly!

Poor Captain! Frozen stiff!

!

We ought to rub him briskly with alcohol . . . if we had some! . . . Ah, I'll bet he has a flask in his hip-pocket.

There . . . I knew it!

Let's see now . . .

Whisky . . . fine

Wait, Captain, not so fast! . . . Don't drink it all!

See, señores . . . Llamas not dead!

Good! . . . Hic . . . Fine! . . . I . . . I . . . I'll f-f-fetch them.

No, no, Captain! I'll go!

Y-you shut up, or I'll s-s-sneeze the mountain down! I . . . I . . . I s-s-started . . . hic . . . all this . . . hic . . . s-s-so I'll f-f-finish it!

But . . .

C-come here, you raggle-taggle ruminants! . . . H-here!

Y-you cushion-footed quadrupeds! . . . They run off as soon as I get near! . . . But I'll fix them!

C-come here you morons, and jump to it! . . .

As if he hasn't done enough damage already!

Look, there! . . . They must have been caught in an avalanche: only two of them left.

All the better: easier for us to deal with them! Come on!

I must be s-seeing things . . . d-down there! . . . The Indians who kidnapped Zorrino!

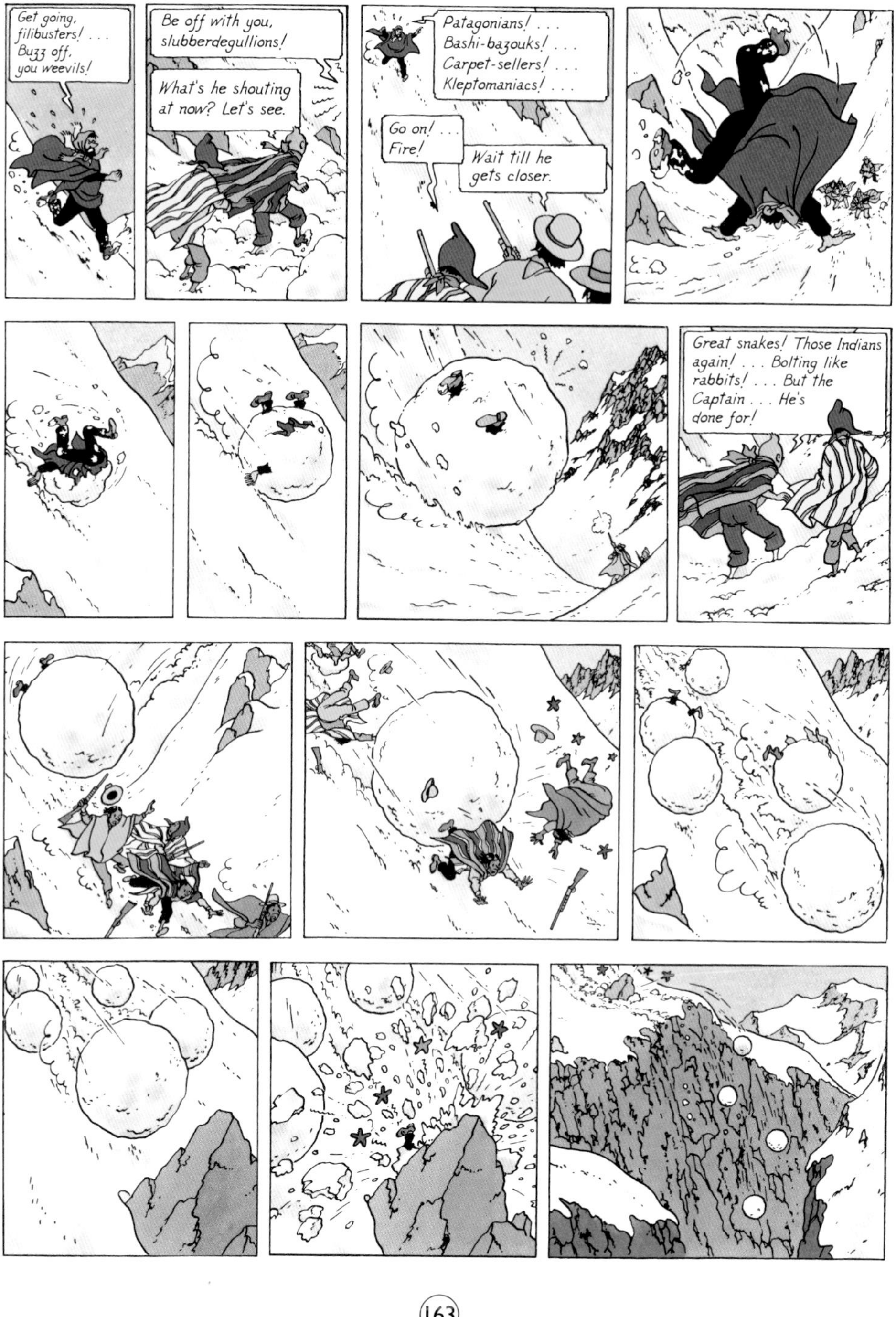
Get going, filibusters! . . . Buzz off, you weevils!
Be off with you, slubberdegullions!
What's he shouting at now? Let's see.
Patagonians! . . . Bashi-bazouks! . . . Carpet-sellers! . . . Kleptomaniacs! . . .
Go on! . . . Fire!
Wait till he gets closer.
Great snakes! Those Indians again! . . . Bolting like rabbits! . . . But the Captain . . . He's done for!

You know, Zorrino, the Captain's guardian angel has a full-time job!

Nothing broken, Captain? . . . That's lucky . . . Well, I reckon we've seen the last of those ruffians . . . Now, let's get back to the path . . .

Yes, yes . . .

I say, where's Snowy? . . . I don't remember seeing him around for quite a while . . . Snowy! . . . Snowy! . . .

Snowy! . . . Snowy!! . . . Where has he got to?

Good old Snowy! You've managed to dig out the Captain's cap.

We've found your cap; that's fine. But I'm afraid we've lost the llamas, and that means no more food, and no more ammunition . . .

No more ammunition?

You needn't worry about that. Look: two boxes of cartridges, here in my pocket.

What a bit of luck! If needs be we can shoot for the pot . . . And take care of that newspaper: we might need it to light a fire.

Many hours later . . .

You see, down there. Tomorrow we come into thick jungle.

Is the Temple of the Sun in the forest?

No, señor, temple still far away. We go through jungle. Then more mountains.

Blistering barnacles! Is there no end to it? I've had about enough of this little jaunt, I can tell you!

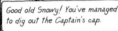

Stop! . . . Look, there's a cave! . . . Why don't we spend the night here?

Perhaps, but . . .

Don't worry. I'll look it over first.

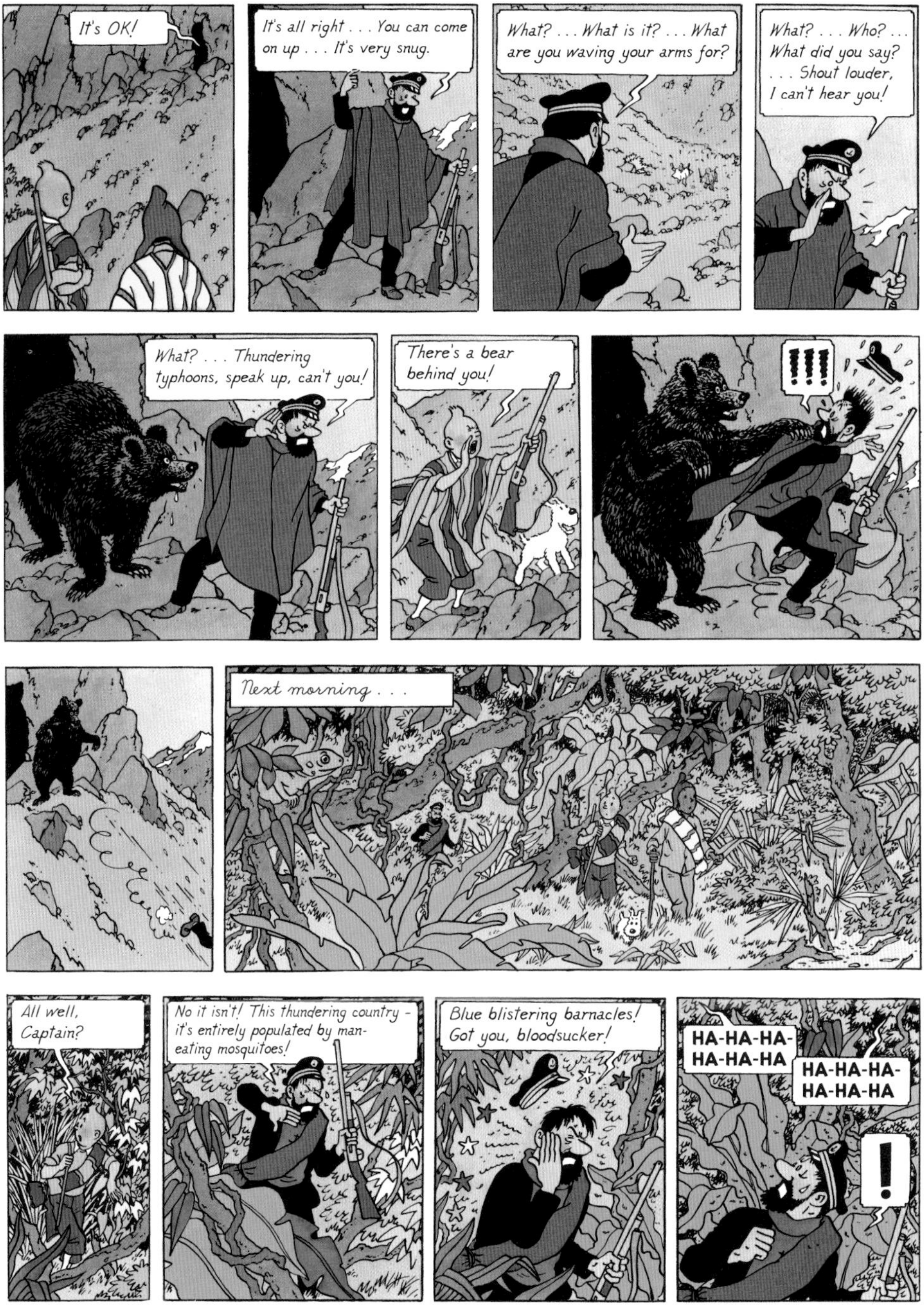
It's OK!
It's all right . . . You can come on up . . . It's very snug.
What? . . . What is it? . . . What are you waving your arms for?
What? . . . Who? . . . What did you say? . . . Shout louder, I can't hear you!
What? . . . Thundering typhoons, speak up, can't you!
There's a bear behind you!
!!!
Next morning . . .
All well, Captain?
No it isn't! This thundering country - it's entirely populated by man-eating mosquitoes!
Blue blistering barnacles! Got you, bloodsucker!
HA-HA-HA-HA-HA-HA
HA-HA-HA-HA-HA-HA
!

HA-HA-HA-HA-

HA-HA-HA HA-HA-HA

Blistering barnacles! . . . Howling monkeys! . . . So you think that's funny, eh, pithecanthropic mountebanks!

Lucky for you we're short of ammunition, otherwise . . .

SPLOSH

!

Billions of blue blistering barnacles . . . All because of those gibbering anthropoids! . . . To blazes with them!

No, just a slight argument with a puddle . . . a mere nothing!

Ah, that's a relief.

HELP! HELP!

?

Listen! Zorrino!

Quick!

BANG

That was a pretty near thing, Zorrino . . .

Señor Tintin, again you save me!

CRACK CRACK CRACK

?

?

CRACK
CRACK
CRACK

Tell me the truth. I can take it. I've been run over by a bus, haven't I?

Rubbish, Captain. It was a tapir.

When tapir in hurry, señor, tapir go straight on. He not worry for things in path. But tapir is not wicked, señor, not hard to tame him.

I'm glad to hear it. All the same, I'll use my gun to tame the next joker who comes along.

I can tell you one thing. Next time I need a nice, restful holiday. I'll know exactly where to come!

Ouch! These beastly mosquitoes!

Here is clearing. Good place to spend night.

Excellent idea . . .

Darkness falls . . .

Next day, at dawn . . .

ZZZZZ

ZZZZZ ZZZZZ
ZZZZZ

!

Mmmm . . . Snowy . . . Go away, Snowy . . . Leave me alone . . .

?

⊚✧☆✺?
?★✦+!
☆⊚ !!

EEK! HELP!

!

Hop it, you four-legged Cyrano!

!

Calm down, Captain: it's only a poor old ant-eater who wanted to say good-morning.

You covered with ants... Him look for breakfast.

The days go by . . .

Very soon, big river . . . We must cross . . .

How? Do we swim?

Bloodsuckers!

You wait here, señor . . . Zorrino come back soon . . .

Right.

How odd. Look at all those tree-trunks floating down the river.

Tree-trunks? Don't you believe it! They're alligators!

Alligators! . . . Good heavens! I could have sworn . . .

A natural mistake . . . They don't fool me.

TINTIN! HELP!

I . . . er . . . thanks, Tintin . . . er . . . you see, I . . .

Quite, Captain! Anyway, he's quite harmless now . . . just like a tree-trunk.

CRACK

It's all right . . . It was only Zorrino breaking a dead branch.

You come, señores. I find canoe.

See . . .

Watch out, shipmates, this is going to be hot! . . . Here they come! They've spotted us!

BANG

BANG

BANG

!

BANG

BANG

Loathsome brutes! Let me polish them off!

No, no! It's a waste of ammunition.

This beastly steaming jungle! . . . Will it never end?

Tomorrow we leave forest, señor Captain.

The following evening . . .

We camp here tonight . . . Up there, in mountains, is Temple of the Sun.

Next morning . . .

Off we go! . . . I say, where did you find that rope?

For certain we need ropes . . . I make them from jungle creepers.

What a torrent! We can't cross here: we'll have to try further up. The Temple of the Sun certainly has good defences!

Two days later . . .

There's nothing for it, Captain: this is the only place . . . You see that spike of rock over there . . . We must try to lasso it with a rope.

Right!

Here goes!

Hooray! Got it!

OK. I've fastened this end to a tree . . . Now, who's first?

Zorrino, with señor Tintin's gun, to test rope!

He's got guts, that boy!

Be careful, Zorrino!

Is OK!

Fine . . . my turn next . . .

Thundering typhoons! You need a cool head for this!

Blue blistering barnacles!

(170)

For heaven's sake, Captain, you'll fall . . . Leave your cap!

And buy another at the local hatter's, I suppose?

Whew! Done it!

Now it's my turn.

Oooh! Let's stop playing Tarzan!

Don't be silly. Snowy . . . We'll be all right . . .

Wooooah!

Help!

Tintin!
Tintin!

He's gone . . . I can't see him . . . But . . . it's impossible . . . He's an excellent swimmer . . . he'll come to the surface.

Not a sign . . . It's all over . . . He's drowned . . . It's too dreadful, I can't believe it . . .

!

Drowned? . . . Drowned? . . . Señor Tintin not dead, is he, Captain?

Alas, Zorrino!

My poor Zorrino. Tintin has gone. We shall never see him again.

Cooee!

?

?

That voice . . . It can't be . . . I must be dreaming . . .

No, no! Is señor Tintin

Captain! Zorrino!

Tintin! . . . Tintin! . . . Is it really you? . . . Where are you?

Wooah! Wooah!

Here, behind the waterfall.

Behind the waterfall? . . . How can you be behind the waterfall?

Come down. You'll see! . . .

?

Climb down . . . Lower . . .

Come closer! . . . Now, watch the foot of the waterfall. I'm going to throw a stone to show where I am.

There!

!   !

You saw it? . . . Good! . . . Now, go up and get the rope. Tie a big stone on the end, and throw it to me . . . I think I've made a very interesting discovery!

Right!

That's tight enough . . . I'll sling it to you.

Splendid!

Secure the end of the rope to a rock. I'll do the same at this end.

OK.

All fast here!

Fine! Now, come on and join me here.

?

W-w-what? . . . We join you? . . . Don't you mean the other way round?

No, no! Hang on tight to the rope and plunge through the waterfall . . . You'll see, it's only a thin curtain of water.

But . . . but . . . you're quite sure . . .

Yes, yes! Come on!

Davy Jones, here I come!

You see?

!

Blistering barnacles! Where are we?

Wait while I call Zorrino . . .

It's incredible! . . . Extraordinary! . . . Amazing! . . . Fantastic!

Your turn, Zorrino!

There you are!

!

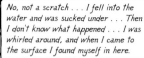
All together again, Zorrino!

Tintin! . . . Oh, Tintin! . . . Zorrino was so afraid. You not hurt?

No, not a scratch . . . I fell into the water and was sucked under . . . Then I don't know what happened . . . I was whirled around, and when I came to the surface I found myself in here.

It seems incredible, but I think I've stumbled on an entrance to the Temple of the Sun . . . so ancient that even the Incas themselves have probably forgotten all about it . . . Anyway, we'll soon see.

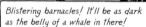
Blistering barnacles! It'll be as dark as the belly of a whale in there!

I thought so too, But I had a look. The rock is covered with some sort of phosphorescence which gives a little light. Shall we go?

No noise, now! . . . Careful! . . . I've got a hunch we're nearly at the end of our journey.

Calculus, here we come!

Where's this leading us?

If we keep going we'll soon see . . .

Now we're in trouble . . . The passage is blocked . . . There's no way of getting through.

The roof-fall was probably caused by an earthquake: they're pretty frequent in South America . . . Anyway, we're sunk now . . . unless . . .

Wooah! Wooah!

I've found the emergency exit!

Snowy seems to be on to something . . . It looks as though there's a way through there. Hold these, Zorrino, I'm going to   try . . .

Any good?   I hope so.

OK?

So far so good . . .

I've just emerged in a sort of grotto . . . I'll see if there's any way of . . . OH!

Heavens! What's up?

I . . . um . . . er . . . Nice day, isn't it?

You . . . er . . . you speak English? . . . No? . . . ¿Habla usted español? No? . . . Well, er . . . parlez-vous français? . . . Oh dear . . .

Great snakes! What a fool I've been . . . of course you don't speak.

Crumbs! Look what's tumbled down . . . the contents of a tomb!

My guess about an earthquake was right . . . Let's see what's beyond . . .

Inca mummies! We certainly are in a tomb!

It might be possible to push this slab over . . . But I can't do it alone . . . I'll call the others . . .

This chap looks pretty poorly.

Hey, Captain! . . . Zorrino! . . . Here, I need your help.

Right, we're coming.

You go first, Zorrino. Then I'll pass you the guns and the ponchos.

You give me guns, señor Captain.

Here you are.

Here guns, Tintin.

Thanks, Zorrino.

Oh! Place of dead men, here!

Yes, Zorrino, there is no other way . . .

It's my turn now . . .

! ? TOOOOT

Crumbs! That noise came from Snowy! What happened?

Golly! Whatever next? A musical bone!

Dead man's flute, Tintin . . . Incas make pipes from bones and put in tomb.

A flute carved out of a tibia . . . And Snowy blew it by mistake . . .

Hey, Captain, where are you?

Blistering barnacles! A tomb! . . . This is cheerful, I must say!

There wasn't any other way through, Captain.

Look here, did you drag me along just to meet these two jolly zombies?

No, no, Captain. There's something else. I'm sure we're nearly there. You see this slab? We must try to push it over. Behind it there might be . . .

What a hope!

Come on now . . . One . . . two . . . three . . . Heave!

Splendid! . . . It moved! . . . Again: one . . . two . . . three . . . Heave!

!

Sacrilege! ... Seize them!

Stand back, anachronisms! ... Keep off, you imitation Incas, you!

Tramps! ... Zapotecs! ... Pockmarks! ...Pithecanthropuses! ... Bashi-bazouks! ... Let me go, you savages!

Good! Now, hold them prisoner until we bring them before the Inca!

Sea-gherkins! ... Ectoplasms! ... Poltroons! ... Politicians! ... Doryphores! ... Terrorists!

Don't cry, Zorrino ... We'll get out of this, you'll see ...

Get out? Easier said than done ... Poor Zorrino!

Hello, what's this at the bottom of my pocket?

Ah, yes, the little coin that Indian gave me in Jauga ... I'd forgotten all about it.

"You still go, then take this ... Very good, help you in danger."

I wonder ... perhaps it's some sort of talisman which protects whoever possesses it ... In that case it might save the life of one of us ...

Look, Zorrino, here's something for you ... Take good care of it: it might be very useful.

You come ... The Inca waits.

Oho! He waits, does he? ... Well, I've got a thing or two to say to his lordship!

Keep calm, Captain! Keep calm, I implore you ...

Great snakes! The Inca!

Look at that Indian on the left ... It's Chiquito, General Alcazar's music-hall partner ... The man I saw on the "Pachacamac".

Strangers, it is our command that you reveal by what trickery you have entered the Temple of the Sun.

I ... er ... Noble Prince of the Sun, we found the entrance quite by chance, when I was swept into a waterfall.

Be that as it may, our laws decree but one penalty. Those who violate the sacred temple where we preserve the ancient rites of the Sun God shall be put to death!

Be put to death! . . . D'you really think we'll let ourselves be massacred, just like that, you tin-hatted tyrant?!

Captain, please! Keep quiet!

Noble Prince of the Sun, I crave your indulgence. Let me tell you our story. We have never sought to commit sacrilege. We were simply looking for our friend, Professor Calculus . . .

Your friend dared to wear the sacred bracelet of Rascar Capac. Your friend will likewise be put to death!

Blistering barnacles, you've no right to kill him! No more than you have a right to kill us, thundering typhoons! It's murder, pure and simple!

But it is not we who will put you to death. It is the Sun himself, for his rays will set alight the pyre for which you are destined.

As for this young Indian who guided these strangers and thus betrayed his race, he will suffer the penalty reserved for traitors! . . . He will be sacrificed immediately on the altar of the Sun God!

Billions of blue blistering barnacles! The first one who touches a hair of that boy's head is a dead duck!

Grrr! . . .

Great snakes! I just remembered! Your medal, Zorrino! . . . Show them!

?

Where did you steal that, little viper?

I not steal, noble Prince of the Sun, I not steal! . . . He give me this medal! . . . I not steal!

And you, foreign dog, where did you get it? Like others of your kind, you robbed the tombs of our ancestors no doubt!

Noble Prince of the Sun, I beg leave to speak . . .

!

It is I, noble Prince of the Sun, who gave the sacred token to this young stranger.

You, Huascar? . . . A high priest of the Sun God, you committed sacrilege and gave this talisman to an enemy of our race?

He is not an enemy of our race, nobel Prince of the Sun . . . with my own eyes I saw him go alone to the defence of this boy, when the child was being ill-treated by two of those vile foreigners whom we hate. For that reason, knowing that he would face other great dangers, I gave him the token. Did I do wrong, illustrious Prince?

No, Huascar, you did nobly. But your action will save only this young Indian, for his life is protected by the talisman.

It will not save the young stranger: by his generosity he forfeited his only safeguard. Our laws are explicit: he will be put to death with his companion.

Nevertheless, I will grant them one favour . . .

I knew it: his bark's worse than his bite!

It is this: Within the next thirty days, they must die. But they may choose the day and the hour when the rays of the sacred Sun will light their pyre.

. . . They must give their answer tomorrow. As for this young Indian, he will be separated from his companions and his life will be spared. But he will stay within our temple until he dies, lest our secrets be divulged.

Now, let the strangers be taken away and kept in close confinement until tomorrow. The Prince of the Sun has spoken!

Well, we're in up to our necks, this time!

I know . . . But I'm glad Zorrino's safe, anyway.

Bunch of savages! . . . What I need is a pipe to calm my nerves . . . Where is it? . . . Ah, got it . . . Hello, what's this?

Oh yes, I remember . . . the newspaper we saved to light a fire.

Well, we shan't be needing that now . . . There'll be a fire all right . . .

But, thundering typhoons, we shan't be lighting it!

How do we get out of here?

These bars, perhaps? . . .
No, they're firmly fixed . . .

Anyway, even if we did manage to shift them, this window overlooks a precipice.

Blistering barnacles! I've lost my matches!

Give me your pipe, Captain. I've got a little magnifying-glass.

A magnifying-glass?

Why, it's alight!

Yes, look . . . that's done it.

Easy as winking! . . . It's amazing! . . . Marvellous!

Marvellous, yes . . . And that's precisely how the Incas will light up their bonfire when they set about roasting us.

. . . Unless they use parabolic mirrors, like Archimedes when he burnt the Roman ships beseiging Syracuse.

My pipe!

My pipe! . . . My poor pipe! . . . Blistering barnacles, it's broken!

Hello, Snowy, what are you doing? Where did you find that paper?

Meanwhile, in Europe . . .

We've searched South America from top to bottom, sir, without result. We lost all trace of Tintin, the Captain and the Professor.

To be precise: we got lost.

We have now decided to undertake a fresh search using entirely new methods. It's the only way: otherwise we have absolutely no hope.

To be precise: we're absolutely hopeless.

I see . . . And what are you new methods?

You must allow us to preserve absolute secrecy, sir . . . "Dumb's the word": that's our motto.

Dowsing, my dear Thompson, like Professor Calculus; that'll put us on their track.

What's this bit of newspaper?

Come on, give it back!

You told me to keep it, remember? In case we needed it . . . to light a fire!

Hello, that's interesting . . . But I wonder . . .

Wooah! Wooah!

!?

Snowy! . . . Here, Snowy! Put that paper down!

Snowy, d'you hear me?

Come here!

Snowy! Snowy! Give me that newspaper!

Snowy! For heaven's sake!

Snowy! . . . Stop fooling around . . . That's enough! . . . Come here!

Golly, I think he really means it!

Ah, with any luck I can put it together.

How very odd! . . . What an extraordinary coincidence!

What a life! I can't even play now.

???!!! ★☆ ◎☀ ★ ★※! +?◎=!!! ❀★:?✕❀⚡ ◎

There, it's mended! Tintin, can you please . . .

!

EUREKA!

!

Tintin, what on earth's going on?

Hip-hip-hooray!

(182)

Captain! Captain! We're saved!

Saved? . . . What do you mean?

Well, you see, I . . . No . . . I don't think I'd better tell you. I could be wrong, and I don't want to raise any false hopes . . .

But I . . .

Listen, Captain: you must trust me, and promise to do exactly as I say, without hesitation. You'll understand later on.

Well, yes, but . . .

Yes? . . . Good: that's a promise! . . . Now we must be patient . . . While we're waiting I'll mend your pipe . . .

Meanwhile . . .

Why, they aren't here! . . . How peculiar! The pendulum definitely indicates that they are somewhere high up.

The next morning . . .

Well, strangers; have you decided upon the day and the hour of your death?

Yes, noble Prince of the Sun . . . I wish . . . we wish to die in . . . er . . . eighteen days' time, at 11 o'clock . . . It is my friend's birthday, and . . .

?

Tintin, you're crazy! . . . You know it isn't . . .

Quiet, Captain! . . . You promised to trust me.

So be it! . . . In eighteen days, at the hour you have chosen, you shall atone for your crime. Guards, take them away. Let them be well treated, and let their least wish be granted!

A few minutes later . . .

Here, señores. You stay in royal apartment now . . .

Now, will you kindly explain what this is all about?

Not yet, Captain, not yet. But you can be sure of one thing: there's nothing to worry about!

Nothing to worry about! . . . Not a sausage! . . . We're only going to be roasted alive in eighteen days' time: apart from that there's nothing to worry about! . . . To be precise, as Thompson and Thomson would say, nothing at all!

Time goes by . . .

Only seven more days . . . Thundering typhoons, we're in a real jam!

Next morning . . .

How can we get out? . . . Who can help us? . . . Zorrino, perhaps . . .

The next day . . .

It's a fine time for gymnastics! Blistering barnacles, here we are with five days to live, and you do morning exercises!

Why not, Captain? One must keep fit.

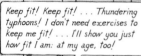

Keep fit! Keep fit! . . . Thundering typhoons! I don't need exercises to keep me fit! . . . I'll show you just how fit I am: at my age, too!

Watch this: a standing jump, feet together, clean over the table.

HUP!

My, my!

!

So you think that's funny, eh?

Only four days left . . .

No one's going to say that I allowed myself to be roasted like a turkey on a spit! . . . We must do something!

You know quite well that's impossible.

Only three days . . .

What can we do, thundering typhoons!?

Round and round . . . he's making me giddy!

Only two days to go . . .

How can you lie there, just lounging around! . . . Billions of blistering barnacles! We must do something!

Trust me, Captain. In two days' time we'll be free.

One day left . . .

It's all over! . . . Nothing to hope for! I never knew things could look so black!

At that moment . . .

According to the pendulum they're very low . . .

Next morning . . .

Only a few hours to live, and all you can do is read that bit of newspaper for the hundredth time!

" . . . The Swiss expedition is on its way to the Western Cordillera in the Andes. It will . . ." The rest is torn away.

Blistering barnacles! If it weren't for these confounded bars I'd soon be out of here!

CRACK BANG BOOM ?

We're free! . . . Tintin, we're free! . . . Come on quickly, hurry! . . . Out!

Don't do it, Captain! You'll break your neck!

Aha! We are just in time!

Thundering typhoons! . . . Too late!

185

The hour has come! You will put on the sacrificial robe.

Me? Put on that Patagonian petticoat? Never!

It is our law. You must obey!

Never! d'you hear? . . . And when I say never, I mean never!

Captain, please . . .

Let him be robed for the sacrifice.

CRASH

Never!

CRACK

BOOM

You think I'm going to be the guy on your bonfire? . . . Never!

Whatever happens, I'm getting out of this madhouse!

!

Nothing broken, I hope, Captain?

Unless I'm much mistaken, there's something very fishy going on.

BOOM BOOM

I wonder what that music is?

If you call it that!

BOOM BOOM BOOM BOOM

Pacharurac - Pachacamac
Viracocha

Cayhinapac Churasunqui Camasunqui

Captain, there's Professor Calculus! . . . Old Cuthbert, after our long search! . . . Here he comes. They're going to tie him up beside us.

Why, Captain! . . . What a delightful surprise! . . . How are you?

Very well, thanks, as you can see!

And you too, my dear Tintin! . . . I'm so pleased to see you again! . . . But tell me, what is all this performance? . . . Where are we?

With the Incas . . .

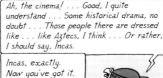

Ah, the cinema! . . . Good, I quite understand . . . Some historical drama, no doubt . . . Those people there are dressed like . . . like Aztecs, I think . . . Or rather, I should say, Incas.

Incas, exactly. Now you've got it.

Yes, their make-up is perfect . . . And look at those dancers: so natural: who'd believe they are acting.

Supposing I'm wrong . . .

Noble Prince, it is the hour of sacrifice!

Meanwhile . . .

According to the pendulum, they should be in a very hot spot . . .

Let the sacrifice begin! ... Let the High Priest of the Sun advance to the pyre!

What's that thing he's got there?

That's the burning glass to set our bonfire alight.

No?

Let me go! You mustn't kill them!

O Pachacamac, blessed lord of the day, maker of earth, god of life, strike now with thine avenging rays!

Stay, Huascar! ... The Sun God will not hear your prayers!

? ?

Grrr!

O magnificent Sun, if it is thy will that we should live, give us now a sign!

Silence, foreign dog! How dare you call upon the Sun?

O God of the Sun, sublime Pachacamac, display thy power. I implore thee! ... If this sacrifice is not thy will, hide thy shining face from us!

Poor Tintin, he's gone off his head!

Not at all: your hat is very chic.

I thank thee, supreme majesty! My prayer is answered; the darkness moves across thy face.

But ... blistering barnacles, he's right! ... Have I gone crazy too? ... It's magic!

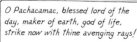
!

(188)

What superb acting! They look genuinely terrified . . . And what an idea to wait for a real eclipse! Brilliant!

An eclipse! . . . An eclipse!! . . . An eclipse!!! . . .

Don't be afraid. An eclipse, it is, that's all Captain.

Wow-ow-woo-ow!

Mercy, O stranger, I implore you! . . . Make the Sun show his light again, and I will grant whatever you desire!

So be it, noble Inca. I accept your word . . . Have no fear: I will entreat the Sun to reappear.

Wow-ow-oowow!

O Sun, lord of the day, show mercy, I pray thee . . . Pity thy children and show thy light once more!

Wow-ow-wow!

By Pachacamac! The Sun obeys him! . . . Quickly! Set them free!

You see now, Captain? The newspaper!

It's . . . it's miraculous!

Supreme lord of the day, we thank thee for thy mercy!

"I've got the sun in the morning . . ." ♫ ♫

A little more dignity, Captain, as befits those who command the Sun!

!

!?*☆★

!!

Meanwhile . . .

Still nothing, yet the pendulum shows they are getting bumped about!

I keep my word, noble strangers: you are free . . . My men will escort you to the foot of the mountains.

Thank you, noble Prince, but I have one further request . . .

In my country there are seven learned men who are still, I imagine, enduring terrible torture because of you. By some means you have them in your power. I beg you to end their suffering.

These men came here like hyenas, violating our tombs and plundering our sacred treasures. They deserve the punishment I have meted out.

No, they did not come to plunder, noble Prince of the Sun. Their sole purpose was to make known to the world your ancient customs and the splendours of your civilisation.

So be it. I think you speak truth . . . It shall be done. Follow me, noble strangers and in your presence I will put an end to their torment.

Each of these images represents one of the men for whom you plead. Here in this chamber, by our hidden powers, we have tortured them. It is here that we will release them from their punishment.

Witchcraft! . . . I can't believe it! . . . But the crystal balls: what were they for?

The crystal balls contained a mystic liquid, obtained from coca, which plunged the victims into a deep sleep. The High Priest cast his spell over them . . . and could use them as he willed.

Now I see it all! . . . That explains the seven crystal balls, and the extraordinary illness of the explorers. Each time the High Priest tortured the wax images the explorers suffered those terrible agonies.

Destroy the images, Huaco!

At that moment, in Europe . . .

What am I doing here?

What's happened? . . . How did I get into hospital? . . .

Where are we, Carling?

That's what I'm wondering, Sanders.

You here, Reedbuck?

Clarkson! . . . What in the world . . .

How did I get here?

Next morning . . .

So you've chosen to stay here, Zorrino . . . We must say goodbye, then. Perhaps one day we shall meet again . . .

Adios, amigo Tintin!

Before you leave us, noble strangers, I too have a favour to ask of you.

I know, noble Prince of the Sun, and you need have no fears about that . . .

I swear that I will never reveal to anyone the whereabouts of the Temple of the Sun!

Me too, old salt, I swear too! . . . May my rum be rationed and my beard be barbecued if I breathe so much as a word!

Me too; I swear I will never act in another film, however glittering the contract Hollywood may offer me. You have my word.

I know I can trust you. Ah, your guides . . .

Blistering barnacles! More llamas!

Perhaps you would like to open one of the saddlebags?

! !

Thundering typhoons! . . . It's fantastic! . . . Gold! . . . Diamonds! . . . Precious stones! . . .

!

We thank you, noble Prince of the Sun, but we cannot accept such magnificent gifts.

Unless you absolutely insist . . .

Oh, they are nothing compared to the riches of the temple! . . . Since I have your promise of silence, come with me . . .

? !

Enter!

Meanwhile . . .

191

See! The treasure of the Incas, for which the Spanish conquerors searched in vain for so long!

It seems unlikely, but there is gold around here somewhere. My pendulum never lies.

Several days later . . .

Now, señores, we leave you here. You take the train and return to your own country . . . Adios, señores, and may the sun shine upon you!

Just a minute . . . Don't go . . .

Will you hang on to my gun for a second?

Of course, but what's up?

Water? . . . The Captain drinking water? . . . I'd never have believed the day would come!

Rum? . . . You think so?

I've nothing against you personally, but that pays a very old debt!

THE END